HOW THE KING OF ELFHAME LEARNED TO HATE STORIES

HOW THE KING OF ELFHAME LEARNED TO HATE STORIES

HOLLY BLACK

ILLUSTRATED BY ROVINA CAI

LITTLE, BROWN AND COMPANY
New York Boston

Little, Brown and Company
Hachette Book Group
1290 Avenue of the Americas, New York, NY 10104
Visit us at LBYR.com

Originally published in hardcover and ebook by Little, Brown and Company in November 2020
First Trade Paperback Edition: May 2024

Little, Brown and Company is a division of Hachette Book Group, Inc.
The Little, Brown name and logo are registered trademarks of Hachette Book Group, Inc.

The publisher is not responsible for websites (or their content) that are not owned by the publisher.

Little, Brown and Company books may be purchased in bulk for business, educational, or promotional use. For information, please contact your local bookseller or the Hachette Book Group Special Markets Department at special.markets@hbgusa.com.

The Library of Congress has cataloged the hardcover edition as follows:
Names: Black, Holly, author. Title: How the king of Elfhame learned to hate stories / Holly Black ; illustrations by Rovina Cai.
Description: First edition. | New York : Little, Brown and Company, 2020. | Series: Folk of the air | Audience: Ages 14 and up. | Summary: Cardan Greenbriar, High King of Elfhame, visits the mortal world to face the troll woman, Aslog of the West.
Identifiers: LCCN 2020022082 | ISBN 9780316540889 (hardcover) | ISBN 9780316540827 (ebook) | ISBN 9780316540872 (ebook other)
Subjects: CYAC: Kings, queens, rulers, etc.—Fiction. | Trolls—Fiction. | Storytelling—Fiction. | Fantasy.
Classification: LCC PZ7.B52878 How 2020 | DDC [Fic]—dc23
LC record available at https://lccn.loc.gov/2020022082

ISBNs: 978-0-316-54081-0 (pbk.), 978-0-316-54082-7 (ebook)

PRINTED IN DONGGUAN, CHINA

APS, 03/26

10 9 8 7 6

For Brian and Drake,
but mostly for Theo

Crooked Forest
Palace of Elfhame
Milkwood
INSMIRE
Lake of Mask
Madoc's Stronghold

Map of the Shifting Isles of
ELFHAME
Locke's Estate
INSMOOR
Tower of Forgetting
INSEAR
INSWEAL
Hollow Hall

A prince of Faerie, nourished on cat milk and contempt, born into a family overburdened with heirs, with a nasty little prophecy hanging over his head—since the hour of Cardan's birth, he has been alternately adored and despised. Perhaps it's no surprise that he turned out the way he did; the only surprise is that he managed to become the High King of Elfhame anyway.

Some might think of him as a strong draught, burning the back of one's throat, but invigorating all the same.

You might beg to differ.

So long as you're begging, he doesn't mind a bit.

How the King of Elfhame Learned to Hate Stories

I

The King of Elfhame Visits the Mortal World

This?" he demands, looking down at the waves far beneath them. "*This* is how you traveled? What if the enchantment ended while Vivi wasn't with you?"

"I suppose I would have plummeted out of the air," Jude tells him with troubling equanimity, her expression saying, *Horrible risks are entirely normal to me.*

Cardan has to admit that the ragwort steeds are swift and that there is something thrilling about tangling his hand in a leafy mane and racing across the sky. It's not as though he doesn't enjoy a little danger, just that he doesn't gorge himself on it, unlike *some people.* He cuts his gaze toward his unpredictable, mortal High Queen, whose wild brown hair is blowing around her face, whose amber eyes are alight when she looks at him.

They are two people who ought to have, by all rights, remained enemies forever.

He can't believe his good fortune, can't trace the path that got him here.

"Now that I agreed to travel your way," he shouts over the wind, "you ought to give me something I want. Like a promise you won't fight some monster just to impress one of the solitary fey who, as far as I can tell, you don't even like."

Jude gives him a *look*. It is an expression that he never once saw her make when they attended the palace school together, yet from the first he saw it, he knew it to be her truest face. Conspiratorial. Daring. Bold.

Even without the look, he ought to know her answer. Of course she wants to fight it, whatever it is. She feels as though she has something to prove at all times. Feels as though she has to earn the crown on her head over and over again.

Once, she told Cardan the story of confronting Madoc after she'd drugged him, but before the poison began to work. While Cardan was in the next room, drinking wine and chatting, she was swinging a sword at her foster father, stalling for time.

I am what you made me, she'd told him as they battled.

Cardan knows Madoc isn't the only one who made her the way she is. He had a hand in it as well.

It's absurd, sometimes, the thought that she loves him. He's grateful, of course, but it feels as though it's just another of the ridiculous, absurd, dangerous things she does. She wants to fight monsters, and she wants him for a lover, the same boy she fantasized about murdering. She likes nothing easy or safe or sure.

Nothing good for her.

"I'm not trying to impress Bryern," Jude says. "He says I owe him a favor for giving me a job when no one else would. I guess that's true."

"I think his presumption is deserving of a reward," he tells her, voice dry. "Not, alas, the one you intend to give him."

She sighs. "If there's a monster among the solitary Folk, we ought to do something about it."

There is no reason for him to feel a frisson of dread at those words, no cause for the unease he can't shake.

"We have knights, sworn to our service," Cardan says. "You're cheating one of them out of an opportunity for glory."

Jude gives a little snort, pushing back her thick, dark hair, trying to tuck it into her golden circlet and out of her eyes. "All queens become greedy."

He vows to continue this argument later. One of his primary duties as the High King appears to be reminding her she isn't personally responsible for solving every tedious problem and carrying out every tedious execution in all of Elfhame. He wouldn't mind causing a little torment here or there, of a non-murdery sort, but her view of their positions seems overburdened with chores. "Let us meet with this Bryern person and hear his tale. If you must fight this thing, there's no reason to go alone. You could take a battalion of knights or, failing that, me."

"You think you're the equal of a battalion of knights?" she asks with a smile.

He might be, he supposes, although there's no telling how the mortal world will affect his magic. He did once raise an isle from the bottom of the sea. He wonders if he ought to remind her of that, wonders if she had been impressed. "I believe that I could easily best all of them combined, in a suitable contest. Perhaps one involving drink."

She kicks her ragwort steed forward with a laugh. "We meet Bryern tomorrow at dusk," she calls back,

and her grin dares him to race. "And after that, we can decide who gets to play the hero."

Having only recently stopped playing the villain, Cardan thinks again of the winding path of decisions that brought him to this unlikely place, here with her, racing over the sky, planning to end trouble instead of making more of it.

II

The Prince of Elfhame Is Rude

Many times in his first nine years, Prince Cardan slept in the hay of the stables when his mother didn't want him in their suite of rooms. It was warm there, and he could pretend he was hiding, could pretend that someone was looking for him. Could pretend that when he was not found, it was only because the spot he'd chosen was so extremely clever.

One night, he was wrapped in a threadbare cloak, listening to the snuffling sounds of faerie steeds, of deer and elk, and even the croaks of great riding toads, when a troll woman stopped outside the pen.

"Princeling," she said. Her skin was the rough bluish-gray of river rocks, and she had a wart on her chin, from which three golden hairs grew. "You are the youngest of Eldred's spawn, are you not?"

Cardan blinked up from the hay. "Go away," he told her as imperiously as he could manage.

That made her laugh. "I ought to saddle you and ride you around the gardens, teach you some manners."

He was scandalized. "You're not supposed to talk to me that way. My father is the High King."

"Better run and tell him," she said, then raised her eyebrows and ran fingers over her long golden wart hairs, curling and uncurling them. "No?"

Cardan said nothing. He pressed his cheek against the straw, felt the scratch of it against his skin. His tail twitched anxiously. He knew the High King had no interest in him. Perhaps a brother or sister might intercede on his behalf if they were nearby, and if it amused them to do so, but there was no telling whether it would.

His mother would have slapped the troll woman and ordered her off. But his mother wasn't coming. And trolls were dangerous. They were strong, hot-tempered, and practically invulnerable. Sunlight turned them to stone—but only until the next nightfall.

The troll woman pointed an accusatory finger at him. "I, Aslog of the West, who brought the giant

Girda to her knees, who outwitted the hag of the Fallow Forest, labored in the service of Queen Gliten

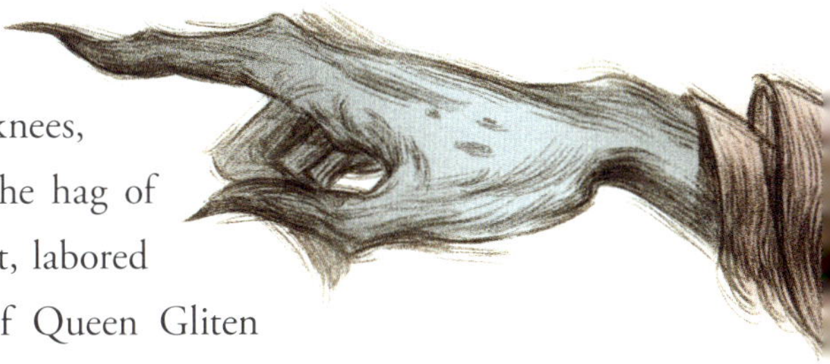

for seven years. Seven long years I turned the stone of her gristmill and ground wheat so fine and pure that loaves of it were famed all over Elfhame. I was promised land and a title at the end of those seven years. But on the last night, she tricked me into moving away from the millstone and forfeiting the bargain. I came here for justice. I stood before Eldred in the place of the penitent and asked for succor. But your father turned me away, princeling. And do you know why? Because he does not wish to interfere with the lower Courts. But tell me, child, what is the purpose of a High King who will not interfere?"

Cardan was uninterested in politics but well acquainted with his father's indifference. "If you think I can help you, I can't. He doesn't like me, either."

The troll woman—Aslog of the West, he supposed—scowled down at Cardan. "I am going to tell you a story," she said finally. "And then I will ask you what meaning you find in the tale."

"Another one? Is this about Queen Gliten, too?"

"Save your wit for your reply."

"And if I don't have an answer?"

She smiled down at him with no small amount of menace. "Then I will teach you an entirely different lesson."

He thought about calling out to a servant. A groom might be close by, but he had endeared himself to none of them. And what could they do, anyway? Better to humor her and listen to her stupid tale.

"Once upon a time," Aslog told him, "there was a boy with a wicked tongue."

Cardan tried not to snort. Despite being a little afraid of her, despite knowing better, he had a tendency toward levity at the worst possible moments.

She went on. "He would say whatever awful thought came into his mind. He told the baker her bread was full of stones, told the butcher he was as ugly as a turnip, and told his own brothers and sisters they were of no more use than the mice who lived in their cupboard and nibbled the crumbs of the baker's bad bread. And, though the boy was quite handsome, he scorned all the village maidens, saying they were as dull as toads."

Cardan couldn't help it. He laughed.

She gave him a dour look.

"I like the boy," he said with a shrug. "He's funny."

"Well, no one else did," she told him. "In fact, he annoyed the village witch so much that she cursed him. He behaved as though he had a heart of stone, so she gave him one. He would feel nothing—not fear, nor love, nor delight.

"Thereafter, the boy carried something heavy and hard inside his chest. All happiness fled from him. He could find no reason to get up in the morning and even less reason to go to bed at night. Even mockery gave him no pleasure anymore. Finally, his mother told him it was time to go into the world and make his fortune. Perhaps there he would find a way to break the curse.

"And so the boy set out with nothing in his pockets but a crust of the baker's much-maligned bread. He walked and walked until he came to a town. Although he felt neither joy nor sorrow, he did feel hunger, and that was enough reason to look for work. The boy found a tavernkeeper willing to

hire him on to help bottle the beer he brewed. In exchange, the boy would get a bowl of soup, a place by the fire, and a few coins. He labored three days, and when he was finished, the tavernkeeper paid him three copper pennies.

"As he was about to take his leave, the boy's sharp tongue found something cutting to say, but since his stone heart allowed him to find no amusement in it, for the first time he swallowed his cruel words. Instead, he asked if the man knew anyone else with work for him.

"'You're a good lad, so I will tell you this, although perhaps it would be better if I didn't,' said the tavernkeeper. 'The baron is looking to marry off his daughter. She is rumored to be so fearsome that no man can spend three nights in her chambers. But if you do, you'll win her hand—and her dowry.'

"'I fear nothing,' said the boy, for his heart of stone made any feeling impossible."

Cardan interrupted. "The moral is obvious. The boy wasn't rude to the innkeeper, so he was given a quest. And because he was rude to the witch, he got cursed. So the boy shouldn't be rude, right? Rude boys get punished."

"Ah, but if the witch hadn't cursed him, he would never have been given the quest, either, would he? He'd be back home, sharpening his wit on some poor candlemaker," said the troll woman, pointing a long finger at him. "Listen a little longer, princeling."

Cardan had grown up in the palace, a wild thing to be cosseted by courtiers and scowled at by the High King. No one much liked him, and he told himself he cared little for anyone else. And if he sometimes thought about how he might do something to win his father's favor, something to make the Court respect him and love him, he kept that to himself. He certainly asked no one to tell him stories, and yet he found it was nice to be told one. He kept that to himself, too.

Aslog cleared her throat and began speaking again. "When the boy presented himself to the baron, the old man looked upon him with sadness. 'Spend three nights with my daughter, showing no fear, and you shall marry her and inherit all that I have. But I warn you, no man has managed it, for she is under a curse.'

"'I fear nothing,' the boy told him.

"'More's the pity,' said the baron.

"By day, the boy did not see the baron's daughter. As evening came on, the servants bathed him and fed him an enormous meal of roasted lamb, apples, leeks, and bitter greens. Having no dread of what was ahead, he ate his fill, for never had he had a finer meal, and then rested in anticipation of the night ahead.

"Finally, the boy was led to a chamber with a bed at the center and a clawed-up couch tucked into a corner. Outside, he heard one of the servants whispering about what a tragedy it was for such a handsome lad to die so young."

Cardan was leaning forward now, utterly captivated by the tale.

"He waited as the moon rose outside the window. And then something came in: a monster covered in fur, her mouth filled with three rows of razor-sharp teeth. All other suitors had run from her in terror or attacked her in rage. But the boy's heart of stone kept him from feeling anything but curiosity. She gnashed her teeth, waiting for him to show fear. When he did not, but rather climbed into the bed, she followed, curling up at the end of it like an enormous cat.

"The bed was very fine, much more comfortable than sleeping on the floor of a tavern. Soon both were asleep. When the boy woke, he was alone.

"The household rejoiced when he emerged from the bedchamber, for no one had ever made it through a single night with the monster. The boy spent the day strolling through the gardens, but although they were glorious, he was troubled that no happiness could yet touch him. On the second night, the boy brought his evening meal with him to the bedchamber and set it on the floor. When the monster came in, he waited for her to eat before he took his portion. She roared in his face, but again he didn't flee, and when he went to the bed, she followed.

"By the third night, the household was in a state of giddy anticipation. They dressed the boy like a bridegroom and planned for a wedding at dawn."

Cardan heard something in her voice that suggested that wasn't how things were going to go at all. "And then what?" he demanded. "Didn't he break the curse?"

"Patience," said Aslog the troll woman. "The third night, the monster came straight over, nuzzling him with a furred jaw. Perhaps she was excited, knowing that in mere hours her curse might be broken. Perhaps she felt some affection for him. Perhaps the curse compelled her to test his mettle. Whatever the reason, when he didn't move away, she butted her head playfully against his chest. But she didn't know her own strength. His back slammed against the wall, and he felt something crack in his chest."

"His heart of stone," said Cardan.

"Yes," said the troll woman. "A great swell of love for his family swept over him. He felt a longing for the village of his childhood. And he was filled with a strange and tender love for her, his cursed bride.

"'You have cured me,' he told her, tears wetting his cheeks.

"Tears that the monster took for a sign of fear.

"Her enormous jaws opened, teeth gleaming. Her great nose twitched, scenting prey. She could hear the speeding of his heart. In that moment, she sprang on him and tore him to pieces."

"That's a terrible story," Cardan said, outraged. "He would have been better off if he'd never left home. Or if he'd said something cruel to the tavern-keeper. There is no point to your tale, unless it is that nothing has any meaning at all."

The troll woman peered down at him. "Oh, I think there's a lesson in it, princeling: A sharp tongue is no match for a sharp tooth."

III

The Prince of Elfhame Hates (Almost) Everything and Everyone

It was not so many years after that Cardan found himself staring at the polished door of his eldest brother's home. On it was a massive carving of a sinister face. As he watched, its wooden mouth twisted up into an even more sinister smile.

You can't frighten me, Cardan thought.

"Welcome, my princes," said the door, swinging open to admit him and Balekin into the ominously named Hollow Hall. As Cardan passed through, a wooden eye gave him a companionable wink.

You can't befriend me, either, he thought.

Balekin led his youngest brother to a room full of furniture covered in velvet and silk. A human woman stood in a corner, dressed in drab gray, her hair streaked with silver and pulled back into a tight bun. A worn leather strap lay across her palm.

"So *I* am supposed to make *you* into a proper Prince of Elfhame," Balekin said, letting his greatcoat, with its bear-fur collar, drop to the floor, kicking it aside to be picked up by some servant, and then settling himself on one of the low and luxuriant couches.

"Or a delightfully improper one," Cardan said, hoping to sound like the sort of younger brother who might be worth taking under Balekin's wing. He led one of the largest and most influential circles at Court, the Grackles, who were committed to merriment and decadence. It was well known that the courtiers who attended the revels in Hollow Hall were indolent pleasure seekers. Maybe there was room for Cardan among them. He was indolent! He liked seeking pleasure!

Balekin smiled. "That's almost charming, little brother. And indeed, you ought to flatter me, because if I hadn't taken you in, you might have been sent to be fostered in one of the low Courts. There are many places where an inconsequential Prince of Elfhame would be the source of much diversion, none of it comfortable for you."

Cardan didn't flinch, but for the first time, he understood that as terrible as things had been up to now, something worse might yet be ahead.

Ever since Dain had tricked him so that the arrow that slew the lover of his father's seneschal seemed to have belonged to Cardan, ever since his mother had been sent to the Tower of Forgetting for his supposed crime and Eldred had refused to hear the truth, ever since he had been sent from the palace in disgrace, Cardan had felt like the boy in Aslog's story. His heart was stone.

Balekin continued. "I brought you here because you are one of the few people who see Dain for what he is and are, therefore, valuable to me. But that doesn't mean you're not a disgrace.

"You will choose clothing suitable to your station and no longer wear garments that are dirty and torn. You will stop scavenging what you can find from the kitchens or stealing from banquets, but sit at a table with cutlery—and use it. You will learn some modicum of swordplay, and you will attend the palace school, where I expect you to do what they ask of you."

Cardan curled his lip. He had been forced into a blue doublet by one of the palace servants and aggressively groomed, down to the combing of the tuft of hair at the end of his tail, but the clothing was old. Loose threads hung from his cuffs, and the fabric of his trousers was worn and thin at the knees. But since it had never bothered him before, he refused to let it bother him now. "All will be as you say, brother."

Balekin's smile grew lazy. "Now I will show you what happens if you fail. This is Margaret. Margaret, come here." He gestured to the human woman with the silvery hair.

She went toward them, although something was unsettling about the way she moved. It was as though she were sleepwalking.

"What's the matter with her?" Cardan asked.

Balekin yawned. "She's ensorcelled. A victim of her own foolish bargain."

Cardan had little experience of mortals. Some came through the High Court, musicians and artists and lovers who had wished for magic and found it. And there were the twin mortal children that Grand General Madoc had stolen and insisted on treating as though they were his own born daughters, kissing them on the tops of their heads and resting his clawed fingers protectively on their shoulders.

"Humans are like mice," Balekin went on. "Dead before they learn how to be canny. Why shouldn't they serve us? It gives their short lives some meaning."

Cardan looked at Margaret. The emptiness of her eyes still unnerved him. But the strap in her hand unnerved him more.

"She is going to punish you," Balekin said. "And do you know why?"

"I am certain you are about to enlighten me," answered Cardan with a sneer. It was almost a relief to know that curbing his tongue wouldn't help, as he'd never been very good at it.

"Because I won't dirty my hands," Balekin said. "Better you experience the humiliation of being beaten by a creature who ought to be your inferior. And every time you think of how disgusting mortals are—with their pocked skin and their decaying teeth and their fragile, little minds—I want you to think of this moment, when you were lower than even that. And I want you to remember how you willingly submitted, because if you don't, you will have to leave Hollow Hall and my mercy.

"Now, little brother, you must choose a future."

It turned out that Cardan didn't have a heart of stone after all. As he removed his shirt and sank to his knees, as he fisted his hands and tried not to cry out when the strap fell, he burned with hatred. Hatred for Dain; for his father; for all the siblings who didn't take him in and the one who did; for his mother, who spat at his feet as she was led away; for stupid, disgusting mortals; for all of Elfhame and everyone in it. Hate that was so bright and hot that it was the first thing that truly warmed him. Hate that felt so good that he welcomed being consumed by it.

Not a heart of stone, but a heart of fire.

Under Balekin's tutelage, Cardan remade himself. He learned to drink a vast variety and quantity of wines, learned how to take powders that made him laugh and fall down and feel nothing at all. He visited the weavers and tailors with his brother, choosing garments with cuffs of feathers and exquisite embroidery, with collars as sharp as the points of his ears, and fabrics as soft as the tuft of his tail—a tail he tucked away, for it showed too much of what he schooled his face to hide. A poisonous flower displays its bright colors, a cobra flares its hood; predators ought not to shrink from extravagance. And that was what he was being polished and punished into being.

And when he returned to the palace dressed magnificently, behaving with perfect deference toward Eldred, shown off by his brother as though he were a tamed hawk, everyone pretended he was no longer in disgrace. Balekin relaxed his rules toward Cardan after that, allowing him to do what he wished so long as he didn't draw the ire of their father.

That spring, Elfhame bustled with preparations for a state visit from Queen Orlagh and had little time to consider an errant prince anyway.

There were whispers that if Orlagh, known for her brutal and swift conquests over her rivals in the Undersea, didn't already control everything beneath the waves, she soon would. And she had announced that she wanted to foster her daughter on land. In the High Court of Elfhame.

An honor. And an opportunity, if someone was clever enough to exploit it.

Orlagh hopes the girl will marry one of Eldred's offspring, Prince Cardan overheard a courtier say. *And then the queen will scheme to make that child the next ruler of Elfhame, so her daughter, Nicasia, may rule land and sea.*

After which, the spouse will likely meet with an accident, put in another.

But if that was what some thought, others saw only the immediate benefits of such an alliance. Balekin and two of his sisters determined they would be the ones to befriend Princess Nicasia, imagining that friendship could change their balance of power in the family.

Cardan thought they were fools. Their father already favored his second-born child, Princess Elowyn. And if she wasn't chosen as his heir, it would be Prince Dain, with his machinations. None of the others had the shadow of a chance.

Not that he cared.

He decided he would be thoroughly unpleasant to the girl from the sea, no matter how Balekin punished him for it. He would not have anyone think he was a part of this farce. He would not give her the opportunity to disdain him.

By the time Queen Orlagh and Princess Nicasia arrived, the great hall was draped in blue cloth. Dishes of cold, sliced scallops and tiny shrimp quivered on trays of ice beside honeycomb and oatcakes. Musicians had taken up playing merfolk songs on their instruments, the music strange to Cardan's ear.

He wore a doublet of blue velvet. Gold hoops hung from his ears, and rings covered his fingers. His hair,

dark as the sloes of a blackthorn, tumbled around his cheeks. When courtiers looked at him, he could tell they saw someone new, someone they were drawn to and a little afraid of. The feeling was as heady as any wine.

Then the procession arrived, clad like a conquering army. They were draped in teeth and bone and skins, with Orlagh leading them. She wore a gown of stingray, and her black hair was threaded with pearls. Around her throat hung the partial jawbone of a shark.

Cardan watched Queen Orlagh present her daughter to the High King. The girl had hair the deep aqua of the sea, drawn back with combs of coral. Her dress was gray sharkskin, and her brief curtsy was that

of someone who had never questioned her own value. Her gaze swept the room with undisguised contempt.

He watched as Balekin swooped to her side, doubtless making light, charming conversation full of little compliments. He saw her laugh.

Prince Cardan bit into one of the raw, wriggling shrimps. It was foul. He spat it onto the packed dirt floor. One of the Undersea guards eyed him, obviously feeling that this was an insult.

Cardan made a rude gesture, and the guard looked away.

He secured himself a large plate of oatcakes slathered with honey and was dunking them into tea when Princess Nicasia wandered over to him. He paused midchew and hastily swallowed.

"You must be Prince Cardan," she said.

"And you're the princess of fishes." He sneered, making sure she knew he wasn't impressed. "Over whom everyone is making such an enormous fuss."

"You're very rude," she told him. Across the floor, he saw Princess Caelia rushing toward them, her corn-silk hair flying behind her, too late to prevent the international incident that was her youngest brother.

"I have many other, even worse, qualities."

Surprisingly, that made Nicasia smile, a lovely, venomous little grin. "Do you now? That's excellent, because everyone else in the palace seems very dull."

Understanding came to him all at once. The daughter of fearsome Orlagh, expected to rule over the brutal, vast depths of the Undersea, had cold-bloodedness for her birthright. Of course she would despise empty flattery and have contempt for the silly fawning of his siblings. He grinned back at her, sharing the joke.

At that moment, Princess Caelia arrived, her mouth open, ready to say something that might distract their honored guest from a wretched younger brother who might not be so tame after all.

"Oh, go away, Caelia," Cardan said before she had a chance to speak. "The sea princess finds you wearisome."

His sister closed her mouth abruptly, looking comically surprised.

Nicasia laughed.

For all the charm and distinction of his siblings, it was Cardan who won the Undersea's favor. It was the first time he'd won anything.

With Nicasia by his side, Cardan drew others to him, until he formed a malicious little foursome who prowled the isles of Elfhame looking for trouble. They unraveled precious tapestries and set fire to part of the Crooked Forest. They made their instructors at the palace school weep and made courtiers terrified to cross them.

Valerian, who loved cruelty the way some Folk loved poetry.

Locke, who had a whole empty house for them to run amok in, along with an endless appetite for merriment.

Nicasia, whose contempt for the land made her eager to have all of Elfhame kiss her slipper.

And Cardan, who modeled himself on his eldest brother and learned how to use his status to make Folk scrape and grovel and bow and beg, who delighted in being a villain.

Villains were wonderful. They got to be cruel and selfish, to preen in front of mirrors and poison apples, and trap girls on mountains of glass. They indulged all their worst impulses, revenged themselves for the least offense, and took every last thing they wanted.

And sure, they wound up in barrels studded with nails, or dancing in iron shoes heated by fire, not just dead, but disgraced and screaming.

But before they got what was coming to them, they got to be the fairest in all the land.

IV

The Prince of Elfhame Gets a Moth Drunk

Prince Cardan wasn't feeling nearly villainous enough as he flew over the sea on the back of an enormous moth late one afternoon. The moth had been his mother's creature, hand-tamed out of the Crooked Forest with honey and wine. Once she was imprisoned in the Tower of Forgetting, the moth languished and was easily tempted into his service by a few sips of mead.

The powder of its wings kept making him sneeze. He cursed the moth, cursed his poor planning, and doubly cursed the middle-aged human woman clutching him too tightly around the waist.

He told himself this was nothing more than a

prank, a way to pay Balekin back for ill treatment, by stealing away one of his servants.

Cardan wasn't saving her, and he would never do this again.

"You know I don't like you," he told Margaret with a scowl.

She didn't reply. He wasn't even sure she'd heard with the wind whipping around them. "You made Balekin a promise, a foolish promise, but a promise all the same. You deserve—" He couldn't get out the rest of the sentence. *You deserved everything you got.* That would have been a lie, and while the Folk could trick and deceive, no untruth could pass their lips.

He glared out at the stars, and they twinkled back at him accusingly.

I am not weak, he wanted to shout, but he wasn't sure he could say that aloud, either.

The sight of the human servants unnerved him. Their empty eyes and chapped lips. Nothing likc the twins from the palace school.

He thought of one of those girls frowning over a book, pushing a lock of brown hair back over one oddly curved ear.

He thought of the way she looked at him, brows narrowed in suspicion.

Scornful, and alert. Awake. Alive.

He imagined her as a mindless servant and felt a rush of something he couldn't quite untangle—horror, and also a sort of terrible relief. No ensorcelled human could look at him as she did.

The glow of the electronic lights shone from the shoreline, and the moth dipped toward them, sending a fresh gust of wing powder into Cardan's face. He was drawn out of his thoughts by a choking fit.

"Onto the beach," he managed between coughs.

Margaret's grip tightened at his waist. It felt as though she was trying to hang on to one of his rib bones. His tail was squashed at an odd angle.

"Ouch," he complained, and was, once again, ignored.

Finally, the moth set down on a black boulder half submerged, its sides scabbed over with white limpets. Prince Cardan slid off the creature's back, landing in a tide pool and soaking his fancy boots.

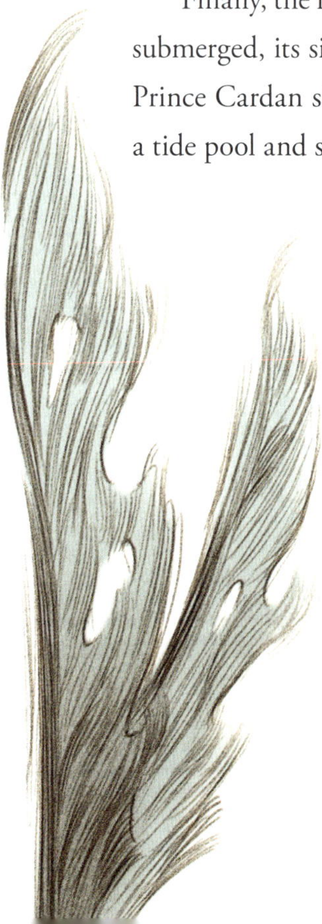

"What happens to me now?" Margaret asked, looking down at him.

Cardan hadn't been sure he'd successfully removed the glamour on her when he'd left Elfhame, but it seemed that he had. "How ought I know?" he said, gesturing vaguely toward the shore. "You do whatever it is mortals do in your land."

She clambered off the moth's back, wading onto the beach. Then she took a deep, shuddering breath. "So this isn't a trick? I can really go?"

"Go," Cardan said, making a shooing motion with his hands. "Indeed, I wish you would."

"Why me?" she asked. She was neither the youngest nor the oldest. She was not the strongest and far from the most pitiable. They both knew the one thing that distinguished her, and it was nothing for either of them to like.

"Because I don't want to look at you anymore," Cardan said.

The woman studied him. Licked her chapped lips.

"I never wanted to..." She let the sentence fall away, doubtless seeing the expression on his face. It had the unsettling effect, however, of mimicking how the Folk spoke when they began a sentence and realized they couldn't speak the lie.

It didn't matter. He could finish it for her: *I never wanted to take a strap to your back and flay it open. It was just that I was glamoured by your brother, because part of Balekin's punishment is always humiliation, and what's more humiliating than being beaten by a mortal? But of course, I* do *hate you. I hate all of you, who took me away from my own life. And some part of me delighted in hurting you.*

"Yes," Cardan said. "I know. Now get out of my sight."

She regarded him for a long moment. The black curls of his hair were probably wind-wild, and the sharp points of his ears would remind her that he wasn't a mortal boy, no matter how he looked like one.

And his wet boots were sinking in the sand.

Finally, she turned away and walked up the cold and desolate beach, toward the lights beyond. He watched her go, feeling wrung out, wretched, and foolish.

And alone.

I am not weak, he wanted to shout after her. *Do not dare to pity me. It is you who should be pitied, mortal. It is you who are nothing, while I am a prince of Faerie.*

He stalked back to the enormous moth, but it wouldn't return him to Elfhame until he went to a nearby general store, glamoured leaves into money to

buy it an entire six-pack of lager, and then poured the booze into a frothing puddle on the ground for the creature to lap at.

V

The Prince of Elfhame Is Mildly Inconvenienced

The odd curve of her ear was what he had noticed first. A roundness echoed in her cheeks and her mouth. Then it was the way her body looked solid, as though meant to take up space and weight in the world. When she moved, she left behind footprints in the forest floor.

Because she didn't know how to glide silently, to disturb no leaf or branch. He felt smug to see how bad she was at even such an easy thing.

It was only later that it disturbed him to think back on the shape of her boot in the soil, as though she was the only real thing in a land of ghosts.

He had seen her before, he supposed. But at the palace school, he really looked. He noted her skirts, spattered with mud, and her hair ribbons, partially undone. He saw her twin sister, her double, as though one of them were a changeling child and not human at all. He saw the way they whispered together while they ate, smiling over private jokes. He saw the way they answered the instructors, as though they had any right to this knowledge, had any right to be sitting among their betters. To occasionally better their betters with those answers. And the one girl was good with a sword, instructed personally by the Grand General, as though she was not some by-blow of a faithless wife.

When she stood up against him, she was so good that it was almost possible to believe she hadn't let him win.

The seeds of Prince Cardan's resentment came full bloom. What was the point of her trying so hard? Why would she work like that when it would never win her anything?

"Mortals," said Nicasia with a curl of her lip.

He had never tried like that for anything in his life.

Jude, Cardan thought, hating even the shape of her name. *Jude.*

VI

The Prince of Elfhame Gets Wet

"Come back with me to the Undersea," Nicasia whispered against Cardan's throat.

They were lying on a bed of soft moss at the edge of the Crooked Forest. He could hear waves crashing along the shore. She was sprawled out in a robe of silver, her hair spread beneath her like a tide pool.

It was a relationship they had fallen into, slipping easily from friendship to kisses with the eagerness of youth. She whispered to him about her childhood beneath the waves, about a foiled assassination that nearly ended her life, and recited poetry to him in the language of the selkies. In turn, he told her about his brother and his mother, about the prophecy hanging

over his head, the one that foretold he would be the destruction of the crown and the ruination of the throne, the one that set his father against him. He could not imagine being parted from her.

"The Undersea?" he murmured, turning toward her.

"When my mother returns for me, come away with us," she said. "Live with me forever in the deep. We will ride sharks, and everyone will fear us."

"Yes," he agreed immediately, thrilled by the idea of abandoning Elfhame. "With pleasure."

She laughed, delighted, and pressed her mouth to his.

Cardan kissed her back, feeling smug at the thought of being consort to the future Queen of the Undersea while the rest of his siblings squabbled over the Blood Crown. He would relish their envy.

Even the prophecy that once seemed to doom him took on a new meaning. Perhaps he *would* destroy Elfhame one day and be a villain above the waves but a hero beneath them. Perhaps all the hatred in his heart was good for something after all.

Princess Nicasia would be his destiny, and her kingdom would be his.

But as he moved to kiss her shoulder, she pushed him away with a grin. “Let’s dive down into the deep,” she said, springing up. “Let me show you what it will be like.”

“Now?” he asked, but she was already on her feet, wriggling out of her dress. Naked, Nicasia ran toward the waves, beckoning him.

With a laugh, he kicked off his boots, following her. He liked swimming and spent hot days in a pond near the palace or bobbing in the Lake of Masks. Sometimes he would float, staring up at the sky and watching the drifting of the clouds. In the sea, he threw his body against the waves, daring them to drag him out with them. If he liked that, then surely he would like this better.

He disrobed on the beach, the water cold on his toes as they sank in the sand. When he waded into the surf, his tail lashed unconsciously.

Nicasia pressed a finger to his lips and said a few words in the language of the Undersea, a language that sounded like whale song and the screeching of gulls.

Immediately he felt a sting in his lungs, an interruption of his breath. Magic.

Orlagh had many enemies in the Undersea, and she sent her daughter to the land not just to firm up the alliance with Elfhame but also to keep Nicasia safe. He wondered if he should remind her of that as he let her lead him out into deeper water. But if she was determined to be daring, then he would be daring with her.

Water closed over his head, making Cardan's dark curls float around him. Sunlight receded. Nicasia's hair became a banner of smoke as she dove, her body a pale flash in the water. He wanted to speak, but when he opened his mouth, water flowed in, shocking his lungs. The magic allowed him to breathe, but his chest felt heavy.

And even though her enchantment protected him, he could still feel the oppressive cold and the stinging of salt in his eyes. Salt that curbed his own magic. And darkness, all around. It didn't feel like the expansiveness of splashing through a pond. It felt like being trapped in a small room.

Give this up and you'll have nothing, he reminded himself.

Silver fish swam past, their bodies bright as knives.

Nicasia swam lower, guiding him until he could see the lights of an Undersea palace in the distance, glowing buildings of coral and shell. He saw a shape that looked like a merrow pass through a school of mackerel.

He wanted to warn her, but when he opened his mouth, he found that speech was impossible. Cardan fought down panic. His thoughts scattered.

What would it truly be like to be a consort to Nicasia in the Undersea? He might be as inconsequential as he was in Elfhame, but even more powerless and possibly even more despised.

The weight of the sea seemed to press down on him. He no longer had a sense of up or down. One was always suspended, fighting against the current or giving in to it. There would be no lying on beds of moss, no barbed words easily spoken, no falling down from too much wine, no dancing at all.

Not even that mortal girl could leave a footprint here without it being instantly washed away.

Then he spotted a glow, distant but sure. The sun. Cardan grabbed hold of Nicasia's hand and made for it, kicking his way to the surface, gasping for air he didn't need.

Nicasia broke the surface a moment later, water flowing from the gills on the sides of her throat. "Are you all right?"

He was coughing up too much water to answer.

"It will be better next time," she told him, searching his face as though she was looking for something, something she rather obviously

didn't find. Her expression fell. "You did think it was beautiful, didn't you?"

"Unlike anything I could have imagined," he agreed between breaths.

Nicasia sighed, happy again. They swam toward the beach, wading onto it and gathering up their clothes.

On their way back toward their homes, Cardan tried to tell himself that he could grow used to the Undersea, that he would learn how to survive there, to make himself consequential, to find some pleasure. And if, as he had floated in the cold darkness, his thoughts turned to the curve of an ear, the weight of a step, a blow that was checked before it could land, that didn't matter. It meant nothing, and he should forget it.

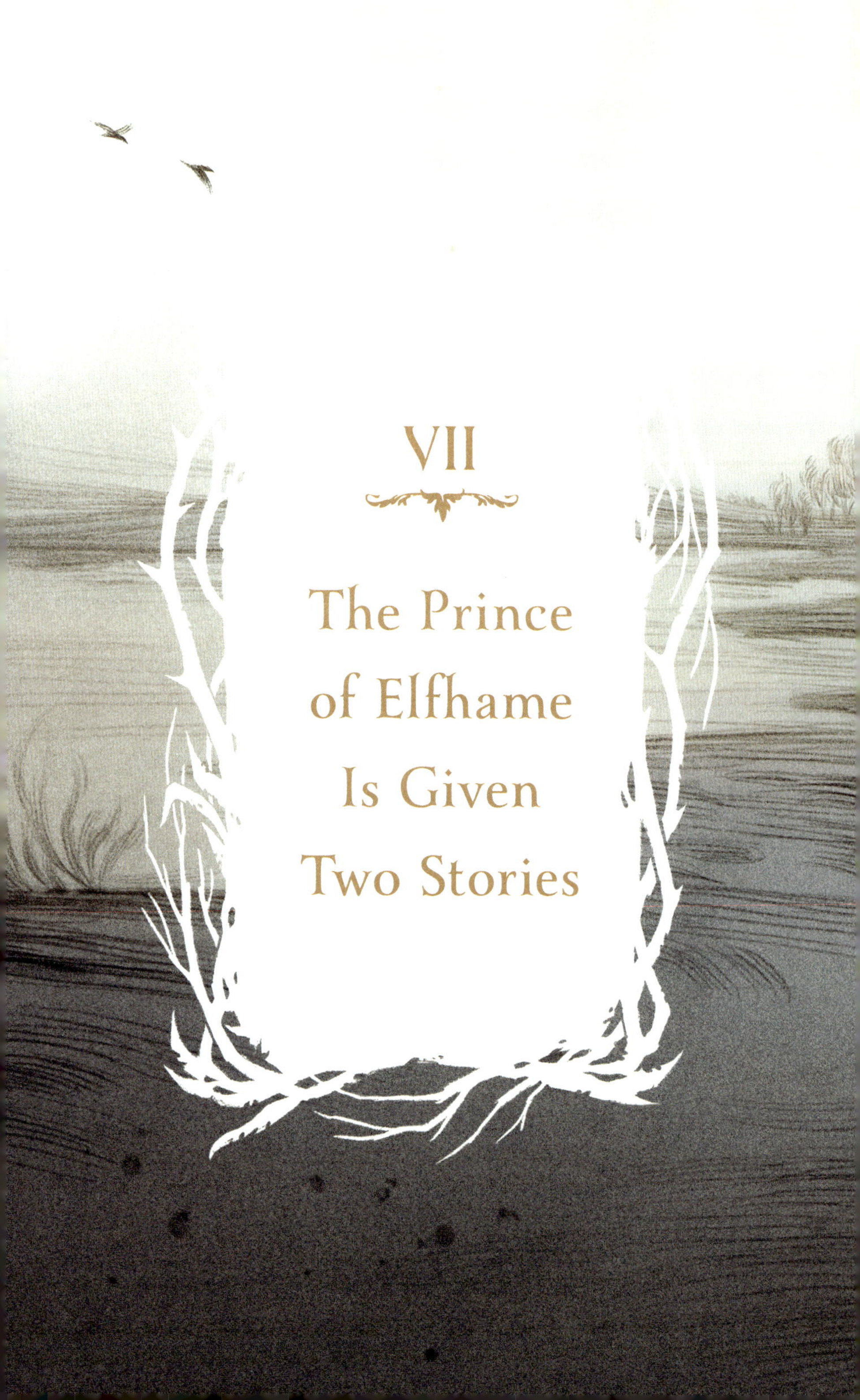

VII

The Prince of Elfhame Is Given Two Stories

As Cardan was no longer in disgrace from the palace, Eldred expected him to come to dinners of state, although he was placed at the far end of the table and forced to endure the glare of Val Moren. The seneschal still believed Cardan was responsible for the murder of a man he loved, and now that Cardan had committed himself to villainy, he took a perverse delight in the misunderstanding. Everything he could do to get under the skin of his family, every vicious drawling comment, every lazy sneer made him feel as though he had a little more power.

Playing the villain was the only thing he'd ever really excelled at.

After the dinner, there was some speechifying, and Cardan wandered off, heading into one of the parlors, on the hunt for more wine. With guests present, Eldred had no way to reprimand him, and, unless he got completely out of hand, it would only amuse Balekin.

To his surprise, however, his sister Rhyia was already there, candles flickering beside her, a book in her lap. She looked up at him and yawned. "Have you read many human books?" she asked.

He liked Rhyia best of his sisters. She was seldom at Court, preferring the wild places on the isles. But she had never paid him any special attention, and he wasn't sure how to behave toward her now that she was.

"Humans are disgusting," he said primly.

Rhyia looked amused. "Are they?"

There was absolutely no reason to think of Jude in that moment. She was utterly insignificant.

Rhyia waved the book at him. "Vivienne gave me this. Do you know her? It's nonsense, but amusing."

Vivienne was Jude and Taryn's older sister and Madoc's legitimate daughter. Hearing her name made him feel uncomfortable, as though his sister could read his thoughts.

“What is it?” he managed.

She put it in his hand.

He looked down at a red book, embossed in gold. The title was *Alice’s Adventures in Wonderland & Through the Looking Glass*. He frowned at it in confusion. It wasn’t what he’d thought a mortal book would be like; he thought they would be dull things, odes to their cars or skyscrapers. But then he recalled how humans were frequently brought to Faerie for their skill in the arts. Flipping the book open, he read the first sentence his gaze fell on.

“I always thought they were fabulous monsters!” said the Unicorn.

Cardan had to flip a few pages back to see whom the Unicorn was discussing. A child. A human girl who had fallen into a place that was apparently called Wonderland.

“This is really a mortal book?” he asked.

He leafed through more pages, frowning.

"Tut, tut, child!" said the Duchess. "Everything's got a moral, if only you can find it."

Rhyia leaned over and pushed a fallen strand of his hair back over one of his ears. "Take it."

"You want *me* to have it?" he asked, just to be sure.

He wondered what he'd done that was worthy of being commemorated with a present.

"I thought you could use a little nonsense," she told him, which worried him a little.

He took it home with him, and the next day he took it to the edge of the water. He sat, opened the book, and began to read. Time slipped away, and he didn't notice someone coming up behind him.

"Sulking by the sea, princeling?"

Cardan looked up to see the troll woman. He startled.

"You recall Aslog, don't you?" she asked with something acid in her voice, an accusation.

He remembered her as something nightmarish and dreamlike from his boyhood. He had half thought he'd invented her.

She was dressed in a long cloak with a pointed end to her hood that curled a bit. She was carrying a basket with a blanket over it.

"I was reading, not sulking," Cardan said, feeling childish. Then he stood, tucking the book under his arm, reminding himself that he was no longer a child. "But I am happy enough to be distracted. May I carry your basket?"

"Someone has learned to wear a false face," she told him, handing it over.

"I had lessons enough," he said, smiling with what he hoped was a sharp-toothed smile. "One from you, as I recall."

"Ah yes, I told you a tale, but that's not how I remember its conclusion," she said. "Walk with me to the market."

"As you like." Her basket was surprisingly heavy. "What's in here?"

"Bones," she said. "I can grind those just as easily as I ground grain. Your father needs to be reminded of that."

"Whose bones?" Cardan asked warily.

"Wouldn't you like to know." Then she laughed. "You were quite young when I told you that story; perhaps you'd like to hear it again with new ears."

"Why not?" Cardan said, not at all sure that he would. Somehow, in her presence, he couldn't manage to behave in the polished, sinister way he'd cultivated. Perhaps he knew how quickly she would see through it.

"Once, there was a boy with a wicked heart," the troll woman said.

"No, that's not right," Cardan interrupted. "That's not how it goes. He had a wicked *tongue*."

“Boys change,” she told him. “And so do stories.”

He was a *prince*, he reminded himself, and he knew now how to wield his power. He could punish her. While his father might not care for him, he would do little to prevent Cardan from being horrible to a mere troll woman, especially one who had come to threaten the crown.

Once, there was a boy with a wicked heart.

“Very well,” he said. “Continue.”

She did, her smile showing teeth. “He put stones in the baker’s bread, spread rumors of how the butcher’s sausages were made with spoiled meat, and scorned his brothers and sisters. When the village maidens thought to change him through love, they soon repented of it.”

“Sounds despicable,” Cardan said, raising an eyebrow. “The clear villain of the piece.”

"Perhaps," said Aslog. "But unfortunately for him, one of those village maidens had a witch for a mother. The witch cursed him with a heart of stone since he behaved as though he had one already. She touched a finger to his chest, and a heaviness bloomed there.

"'You will feel nothing,' she told him. 'Not love nor fear nor delight.' But instead of being horrified, he laughed at her.

"'Good,' the boy said. 'Now there is nothing to hold me back.' And with that, he set out from home to seek his fortune. He thought that with a heart of stone, he could be worse than ever before."

Cardan gave Aslog a sidelong glance.

She winked at him and cleared her throat. "After traveling for a day and a night, he came to a tavern, where he waited for a drunk to stagger out, then robbed him. With that coin, he purchased a meal, a room for the night, and a round of drinks for the locals. This made them think so well of him that they soon told him all the interesting news of the area.

"One story was that of a rich man with a daughter he wanted to marry off. To win her, one must spend three nights with the girl and show no sign of fear. The men at the tavern speculated long and lewdly over what that might mean, but all the boy cared about was that he feared nothing and needed money. He stole a horse and rode on to the rich man's house, where he presented himself."

"I told you the moral of the tale was obvious last time, but don't you think this is a little much?" Cardan said. "He's awful, and so his punishment is getting eaten."

"Is it?" asked Aslog. "Listen a little longer."

The market was in sight, and Cardan thought that when they got there, he would buy a wineskin and drink the whole thing in one go. "I suppose I must."

She laughed. "There's the princeling I remember! Now, the rich man explained his daughter was under a curse—and if the boy could survive three nights with her, the curse would be broken. 'Then you may marry her and have all I possess,' the man told the boy. And looking

around the massive estate, the boy thought he could be satisfied with that.

"But as evening came on, although the boy wasn't afraid, he was disturbed to feel nothing at all. He ought to be nervous, at least. Though he had been served an enormous meal at the rich man's table, with food and drink finer than he had ever tasted, it had given him no pleasure. For the first time, the witch's curse haunted him. No matter what happened, he could never find happiness. And perhaps it was no good thing that he couldn't feel fear.

"But he was committed to his course and so allowed himself to be led into a chamber with a curtained bed. On the wall were scrapes disturbingly like claw marks. The boy went to a low bench and waited as the moon rose outside the window. Finally, she entered, a monster covered in fur and her mouth filled with three rows of razor-sharp teeth. He would have screamed or run and fled, but for his heart of stone. She gnashed her teeth, waiting for him to show fear. But instead he climbed up into the bed and beckoned for her to join him so that he could swive her."

"This is most certainly not the story you told me when I was nine," said Prince Cardan, eyebrows rising.

"How better to show that he had no fear?" The troll woman's smile was all teeth.

"Ah, but without the terror, surely it had not half the savor," he returned.

"I think that says more about you, princeling, than about the boy," Aslog said, resuming her tale. "The next morning, the rich man's household was in an uproar when they found the boy asleep in bed, apparently unharmed. He was brought breakfast and a fresh suit of clothes, finer than any he'd ever owned, but he felt so little pleasure from the wearing of them that they might as well have been rags. All day he wandered the grounds, looking for where the monster spent her days, but he didn't spot her.

"The second night went much as the first. She roared in his face, but again he didn't flee. And when he went to the bed, she followed.

"By the third night, the household was in a state of giddy anticipation. They dressed the boy like a bridegroom and planned for a wedding at dawn."

They had arrived at the edge of the shops. Cardan handed the basket back to her, glad to be rid of it. "Well, I'll be off. We both know what happens on the third night. The boy's curse is broken, and he dies."

"Oh no," said the troll woman. "The rich man makes the boy his heir."

He frowned. "No, that's not right—"

She cut him off. "On the third night, the boy went into the bedchamber, expecting that all would proceed as it had before. When the monster came into the room, he beckoned her to the bed. But a moment later, another monster slunk in, this one larger and stronger than the first.

"You see, the rich man hadn't told the boy the whole truth about the curse. His daughter had spurned a witch's son and been cursed by the witch, a curse forcing the girl to take for her husband anyone—no matter how poor or hideous—who could spend three nights with her and show no fear. But what the witch didn't know was that the girl had rejected the son out of fear for him. For she loved the son, and her father had threatened to have him slain if they wed.

"Now, the witch's son knew only a little magic, but he knew a great deal about the heart of the rich man's daughter. And so, when rumors came to him that someone was going to break the curse, he knew he must act immediately. He could not break the curse, but he did know how to bring a curse down on himself.

"And so he made himself a monster twin to hers and rushed at the boy.

"The boy's back slammed against the wall, and he felt something crack in his chest. His curse was broken. He felt remorse for at least a few of the things he'd done. And he was filled with a strange and tender love for her, his cursed bride.

"'Stay back,' the boy shouted at the new monster, tears wetting his cheeks. He grabbed up a poker from before the fire.

"But before he could strike, the two monsters went out the window, flying into the night. He watched them go, his heart no longer stone, but heavier than before. The next morning, when he was discovered, he went to the rich man and told him the tale. And since the man's

only daughter was gone, he declared that the boy should be his heir and inherit all his lands."

"Even though he was terrible?" Cardan said. "Because they were both terrible? Don't ask me the lesson, because I don't know it and I can't imagine there is one."

"No?" Aslog inquired. "It's simply this. A heart of stone can still be broken."

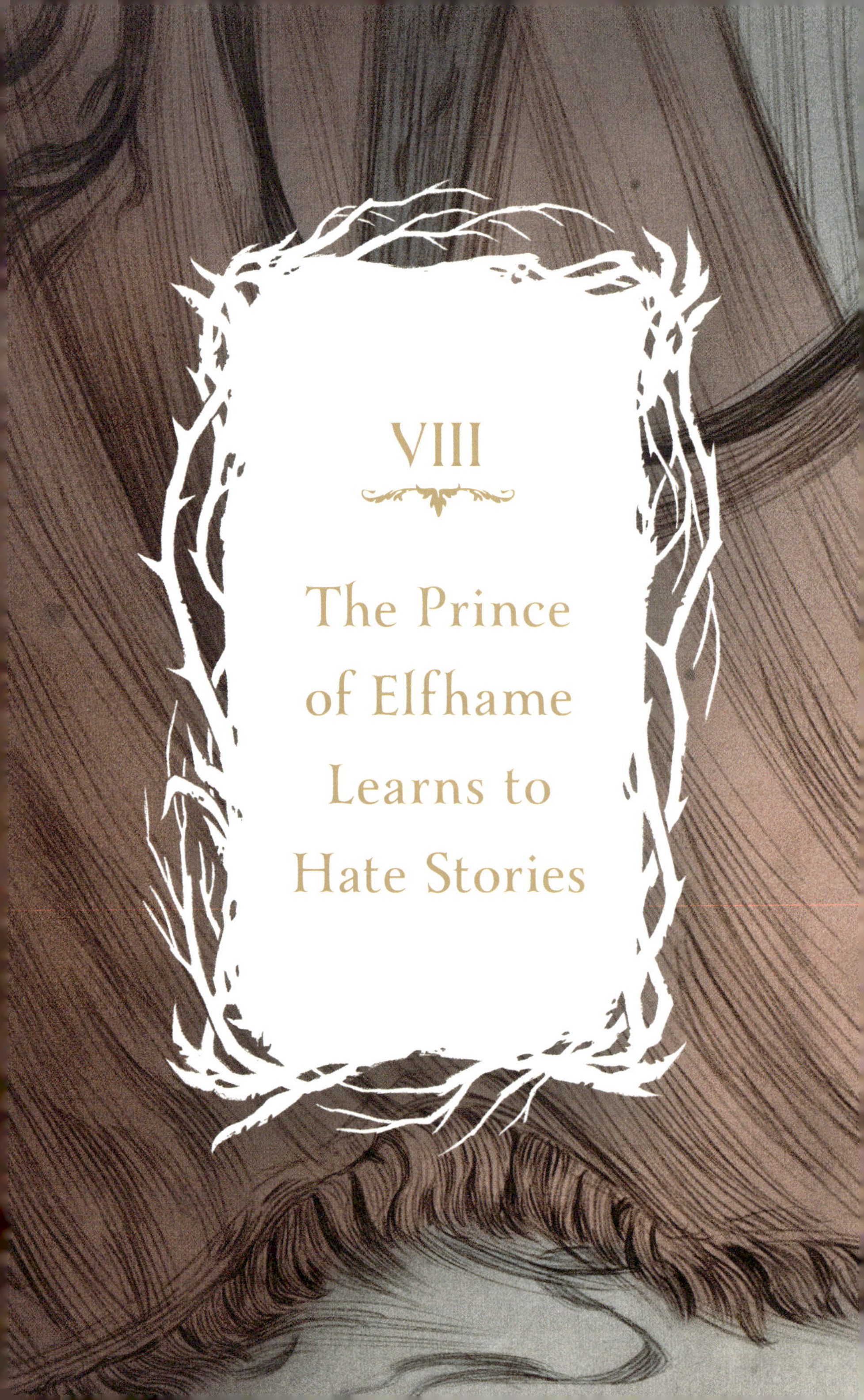

VIII

The Prince of Elfhame Learns to Hate Stories

If Aslog's tale was an ill omen, Prince Cardan did his best to push it away with overindulgence, merriment, and an absolute refusal to think about the future.

It was working a treat when Prince Cardan awoke on a rug in the parlor of Hollow Hall. Late-afternoon sunlight streamed in through the window. He was fully dressed, stank of wine, and felt light-headed in a way that suggested he might yet be drunk.

He was not the only one to have fallen asleep on the floor. Near him, a lilac-skinned courtier in a ball gown with tattered hems slumbered on, her thin wings twitching on her back. And next to her sprawled a trio of pixies, gold dust in their hair. On the couch was a

troll, with what looked like blood crusted around his mouth.

Prince Cardan tried to recall the party, but what he mostly remembered was Balekin tipping a goblet against his lips.

The night began coming back to him in pieces. Balekin had encouraged Cardan to bring his friends to his latest revel. Usually, they spent their riotous evenings drinking wine in the moonlight and coming up with such schemes as might amuse them and horrify the populace.

Your little Grackle protégés, Balekin had called them.

Cardan was skeptical about the invitation, as his eldest brother was most generous when he would somehow become the greatest beneficiary of his largess. But Valerian and Locke were eager to compete with the legendary debauchery of the Grackles, and Nicasia was looking forward to mocking everyone, so there was no dissuading them.

She had arrived in a gown of black silk beneath a cage of fish bones and shells, her deep aquamarine hair caught up in a crown of coral. One look at her, and at his brother, and Cardan couldn't help recalling how Balekin had once planned to win influence through her favor.

He might have worried that his brother still planned something like that. But she had assured him many times that she considered all of Elfhame beneath her, all of Elfhame save for Cardan.

Valerian arrived soon after, and Locke shortly followed. They took to Balekin's form of merriment as ticks to blood. Much wine was poured. Courtiers shared gossip and flirtations and promises for the evening ahead. There was a brief spate of declaiming erotic poetry. Powders were pressed on Cardan's tongue, and he passed them to Nicasia with a kiss.

As dawn broke, Cardan experienced a vast delight with the world and everyone in it. He even felt an expansiveness toward Balekin, a gratitude for being taken in and remade in his eldest brother's image, no matter how harsh his methods. Cardan went to pour another goblet of wine with which to make a toast.

Across the room, he saw Locke sit down beside Nicasia on one of the low velvet couches, close enough that his thigh pressed against hers, and then turned to whisper in her ear. She glanced over, a guilty look flashing across her features when she saw Cardan notice.

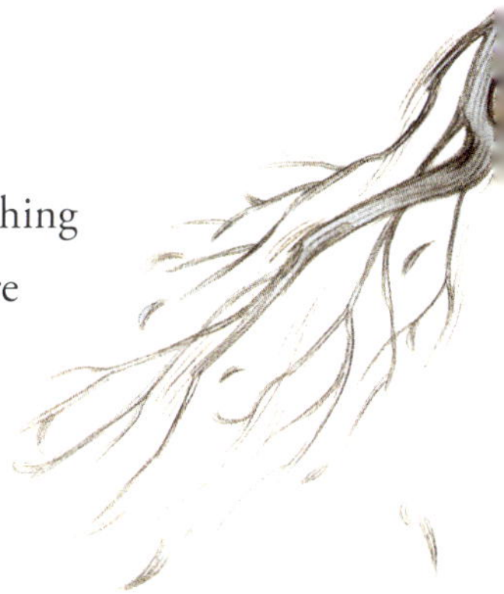

But it was easy to let such a little thing slip from his thoughts as the evening wore on. Revelry is inherently slippery; part of its munificence is an easing of boundaries. And there were plenty of entertainments to distract him.

A treewoman got up on a table to dance. Her branches brushed against the chandeliers, her knothole eyes were closed, and her bark-covered fingers waved in the air. She took swigs from a bottle.

"It's too bad Balekin didn't invite the Duarte girls," said Valerian with a curled lip, his gaze on an ensorcelled human taking a silver platter of grapes and split-open pomegranates to the table. "I would relish the chance to demonstrate their true place in Elfhame."

"Oh no, I rather like them," Locke said. "Especially the one. Or is it the other?"

"The Grand General would mount your head on a wall," Nicasia informed him, patting his cheek.

"A very fine head," he informed her with a wicked grin. "Suitable for mounting."

Nicasia cut her gaze toward Cardan and said no more. Her expression was a careful blank. He marked that, when he wouldn't have marked their words.

Cardan tipped back his goblet and drank it to the dregs, ignoring the sourness in his stomach. The evening quickly became a blur.

He recalled the treewoman crashing through a table. Sap leaked out of her open mouth as Valerian studied her with an odd, cruel expression.

A hob played a lute strung with another reveler's hair.

Sprites swarmed around a spilled jug of mead.

Cardan stood in the gardens, staring up at the stars.

Then he woke on the rug. Looking around the room, he didn't spot anyone he knew. He stumbled up the stairs and into his room.

There he found Locke and Nicasia curled up on the rug before the dying fire. They were wrapped in the tapestry blanket from his bed. Her black silk gown had been discarded in a shining puddle, the cage she'd worn over it now tucked half

underneath the bed. Locke's white coat was spread across the wooden planks of the floor.

Nicasia's head rested on Locke's bare chest. Fox-red hair stuck to his cheek with sweat.

As Cardan stared at them, a rush of blood heated his cheeks, and the pounding in his head grew so loud that it momentarily drowned out thought. He looked at their tangled bodies, at the glowing embers in the grate, at the half-finished work for the palace tutors that was still on his desk, sloppy blotches of ink dotting the paper.

Cardan ought to have been the boy with the heart of stone in Aslog's story, but somehow he had let his heart turn to glass. He could feel the shattered shards of it lodged in his lungs, making his every breath painful.

Cardan had trusted Nicasia not to hurt him, which was ridiculous, since he well knew that everyone hurts one another and that the people you loved hurt you the most grievously. Since he was well aware that they both took delight in hurting everyone else that they could, how could he have thought himself safe?

He knew he had to wake them, sneer, and behave as though it didn't matter. And since his only true talent so far had ever been in awfulness, he trusted that he could manage it.

Cardan nudged Locke with a booted foot. It wasn't quite a kick, but it wasn't far from one, either. "Time to get up."

Locke's eyelashes fluttered. He groaned, then stretched. Cardan could see the calculation flash in his eyes, along with something that might have been fear. "Your brother throws quite the revel," he said with a deliberately casual yawn. "We lost track of you. I thought you might have gone off with Valerian and the treewoman."

"And why would you suppose that?" Cardan asked.

"It seemed you were attempting to outdo each other in *excess*." Locke gestured expansively, a false smile on his face. One of Locke's finest qualities was his ability to recast all their lowliest exploits as worthy of a ballad, told and retold until Cardan could almost believe that staggeringly better or thrillingly worse version of events. He could no more lie than any of the Folk, but stories were the closest thing to lies the Folk could tell.

And perhaps Locke hoped to make a story of this moment. Something they could laugh over. Perhaps Cardan ought to let him.

But then Nicasia opened her eyes. And at the sight of Cardan, she sucked in her breath.

Tell me it means nothing, that it was just a bit of fun, he thought. *Tell me and everything will be as it was before. Tell me and I will pretend along with you.*

But she was silent.

"I would have my room," Cardan said, narrowing his eyes and assuming his most superior pose. "Perhaps you two might take whatever this is elsewhere."

Part of him thought she would laugh, having known him before he perfected his sneer, but she shrank under his gaze.

Locke stood up, putting on his pants. "Oh, don't be like that. We're all friends here."

Cardan's practiced demeanor went up in smoke. He became the snarling feral child that had prowled the palace, stealing from tables, unkempt and unloved. Launching himself at Locke, he bore him to the floor. They collapsed in a heap. Cardan punched, hitting Locke somewhere between the eye and the cheekbone.

"Stop telling me who I am," he snarled, teeth bared. "I am tired of your stories."

Locke tried to knock Cardan off him. But Cardan had the advantage, and he used it to wrap his hands around Locke's throat.

Maybe he really was still drunk. He felt giddy and dizzy all at once.

"You're going to really hurt him!" Nicasia shouted, hitting Cardan's shoulder and then, when that didn't work, trying to haul him off the other boy.

Locke made a wordless sound, and Cardan realized he was pressing so tightly on his windpipe that he couldn't speak.

Cardan dropped his hands away.

Locke choked, gasping for air.

"Create some tale about this," Cardan shouted, adrenaline still fizzing through his bloodstream.

"Fine," Locke finally managed, his voice strange. "Fine, you mad, hedge-born coxcomb. But you were only together out of habit; otherwise, it wouldn't have been so easy to make her love me."

Cardan punched him. This time, Locke swung back, catching Cardan on the side of the head. They rolled around, hitting each other, until Locke scuttled back and made it to his feet. He ran for the door, Cardan right behind.

"You are both fools," Nicasia shouted after them.

They thundered down the stairs, nearly colliding with Valerian.

His shirt was singed, and he stank of smoke. “Good morrow,” he said, apparently not noticing the bruises rising on Locke’s face or how the sight of him had brought them all up short. “Cardan, I hope your brother won’t be angry. I’m afraid I may have set one of the guests on fire.”

Cardan had no time to react or to even find out if someone died before Nicasia grabbed his arm. "Come with me," she said, dragging him into a parlor where a faun was spread out on a divan. The faun sat up at the sight of them.

"Get out," she commanded, pointing at the door. With a single look at her face, the faun left, his hooves clacking on the stone floor.

Then she spun on Cardan. He folded his arms over his chest protectively.

"I'm a little glad you hit him," Nicasia said. "I'm even glad you found us. You ought to have known from the first, and it was only cowardice that kept me from telling you."

"Do you suppose that I am glad as well? I'm not." Cardan was having difficulty assuming his previous reserve, what with his left ear ringing from the blow Locke landed, his knuckles burning from the punches he'd thrown, and Nicasia before him.

"Forgive me." She looked up, a little smile at the corners of her mouth. "I do care for you. I always shall."

He wanted to ask if Locke was right, if friendship had stolen the thrill from being lovers. But looking at her, he knew the answer. And he knew the only way he could possibly keep his dignity.

"You have cast your lot with him," he said. "There is nothing to forgive. But if you regret it, do not think that you will be able to call me back to your side like some forgotten plaything you mislaid for a while."

Nicasia looked at him, a little frown forming between her brows. "I wouldn't—"

"Then we understand each other." Cardan turned and stalked from the parlor.

Valerian and Locke had disappeared from the hall.

To Cardan, there seemed little purpose to do anything but resume drinking before he properly sobered up. The shouting and punching had disturbed enough revelers to wake them. Most were glad to join Cardan in new bouts of merriment.

He licked golden dust from collarbones and drank strong, grass-scented liquor from the belly button of a phooka. By the time it occurred to him that he had missed school, he had been drunk for three days and consumed enough powders and potions to have been awake for most of that time.

If he stank of wine before, now he reeked of it, and if he'd felt light-headed then, now he was reeling.

But it seemed to him that he ought to present himself to his tutors and show the children of the

Gentry that no matter what they'd heard, he was fine. In fact, he had seldom felt so fine before in his life.

He staggered through the hall and out the door.

"My prince?" The door's wooden face was the picture of distress. "You're not truly going out like that, are you?"

"My door," Cardan replied. "I most certainly am."

He promptly fell down the front steps.

At the stables, he began to laugh. He had to lie down in the hay he was laughing so hard. Tears leaked out of his eyes.

He thought of Nicasia and Locke and dalliances and stories and lies, but it all jumbled together. He saw himself drowning in a sea of red wine from which an enormous moth was steadily drinking; saw Nicasia with a fish's head instead of a tail; saw his hands around Dain's throat; saw Margaret looming over him with a strap, giggling, as she transformed into Aslog.

Dizzily, he climbed up onto the back of a horse. He ought to tell Nicasia she was no longer welcome on the land, that he, son of the

High King, was *disinviting* her. And he was going to exile Locke. No, he was going to find someone to put a *curse* on Locke so that he vomited eels every time he spoke.

And then he was going to tell the tutors and everyone else at the palace exactly how wonderful he felt.

Riding was a blur of forest and path. At one point, he found himself hanging off the side of the saddle. He almost slipped into a thicket of briars before he managed to pull himself upright again. But nearly falling made him briefly feel clearheaded.

He looked out at the horizon, where the blue sky met the black sea, and he thought of how he no longer would spend his days beneath it.

You hated it there, he reminded himself.

But his future stretched in front of him, and he no longer saw any path through it.

He blinked. Or closed his eyes for longer than a blink. When he opened them, he was at the edge of the palace grounds. Soon grooms would come and lead his horse to the stables, leaving him to stagger onto the green. But the distance seemed too great. No, digging his heels into the flanks of his horse, he careened toward where all the other children of the Gentry demurely waited to get their lessons.

At the sound of the horse's hoofbeats, a few got to their feet.

"Ha!" he shouted at them as they scattered. He chased after several, then veered widdershins to run down others who'd thought themselves safe. Another laugh bubbled up.

A few more turns and he spotted Nicasia, standing beside Locke, sheltered beneath the canopy of a tree. Nicasia looked horrified. But Locke couldn't hide his utter delight at this turn of events.

Whatever flame lived inside Cardan, it burned only hotter and brighter.

"Lessons are suspended for the afternoon, by royal whim," he announced.

"Your Highness," said one of his tutors, "your father—"

"Is the High King," Cardan finished for him, pulling on the reins and pressing with his thighs so the horse advanced. "Which makes me the prince. And you one of my subjects."

"*A* prince," he heard someone say under her breath. He glanced over to see the Duarte girls. Taryn was clutching her twin sister's hand so hard that her nails were dug into Jude's skin. He was certain she wasn't the one who'd spoken.

He turned his gaze on Jude.

Curls of brown hair hung to her shoulders. She was dressed in a russet wool doublet over a skirt that showed a pair of practical brown boots. One of her hands was at her hip, touching her belt, as though she thought he might draw the weapon sheathed there. The idea was hilarious. He certainly hadn't buckled on a sword in preparation for coming here. He wasn't even sure he could stay standing long enough to swing, and he had only beaten her when he was sober because she let him.

Jude looked up at him, and in her eyes, he recognized a hate big enough and wide enough and deep enough to match his own. A hate you could drown in like a vat of wine.

Too late to hide it, she lowered her head in the pretense of deference.

Impossible, Cardan thought. *What had she to be angry about, she who had been given everything he was denied?* Perhaps he had imagined it. Perhaps he wanted to see his reflection on someone else's face and had perversely chosen hers.

With a whoop, he rode in her direction, just to watch her and her sister run. Just to show her that if she did hate him, her hatred was as impotent as his own.

The way back to Hollow Hall took far longer than the ride there. Somehow he became lost in the forest and let his horse wander through the Milkwood, branches tearing at his clothes and black-thorned bees buzzing angrily around him.

"My prince," the door said as he stumbled up the steps, "news of your escapade has reached your brother. You might want to delay—"

But Cardan only laughed. He even laughed when Balekin ordered him into his office, expecting another servant and another strap. But it was only his brother.

"I have seen enough of your maudlin display to understand that you have lost some favor with Nicasia?" Balekin said.

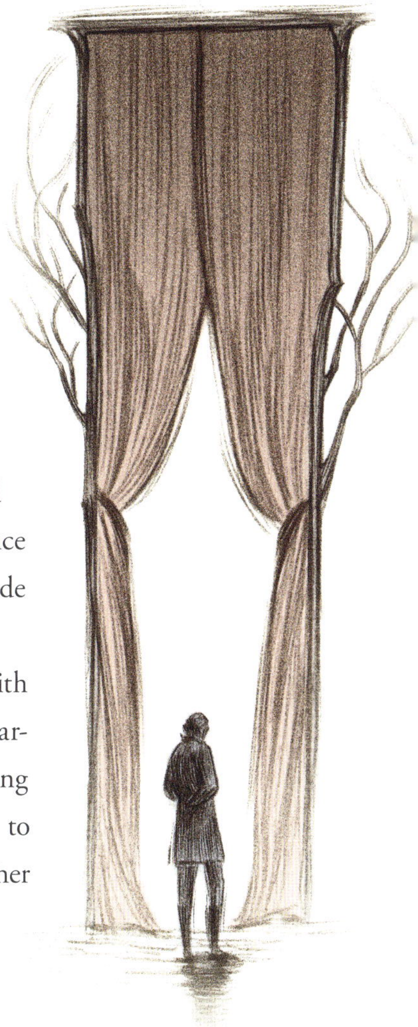

Since he wasn't sure he could stay upright, Cardan sat. And since a chair wasn't immediately beside him, he sat on the floor.

"Do not invest a dalliance with greater significance than it warrants," Balekin went on, coming around from behind his desk to peer down at his younger brother not entirely unsympathetically. "It is a mere nothing. No need for dramatics."

"I am nothing," Cardan said, "if not dramatic."

"Your relationship with Princess Nicasia is the closest thing to power that you have," Balekin said. "Father overlooks your excesses to keep peace with the Undersea. Do you think he would tolerate your behavior otherwise?"

"And I suppose *you* need me to have influence with Queen Orlagh for something or another," Cardan guessed.

Balekin didn't deny it. "Make sure she comes back to you when she tires of this new lover. Now take yourself to bed—*alone*."

As Cardan crawled up the steps, his head ringing with hoofbeats, he thought of how he'd vowed not to be one of the fools groveling for the affections of some princess of the Undersea and of how, if he wasn't careful, that was exactly what he would become.

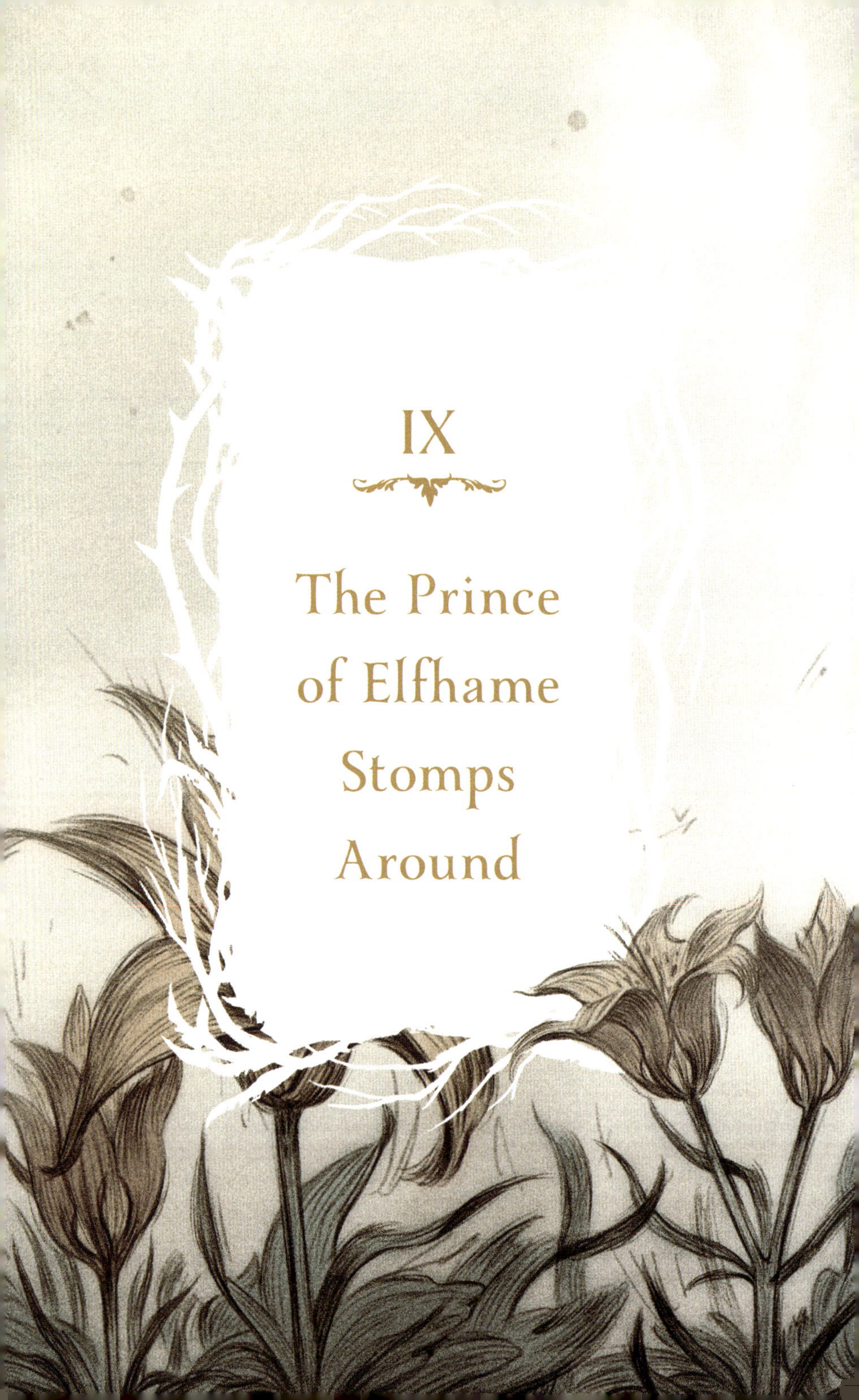

IX

The Prince of Elfhame Stomps Around

Cardan had his polished boots resting on a rock and his head pillowed on the utterly ridiculous mortal book he'd been reading. Since the one with the girl and the rabbit and the bad queen, he'd discovered he had a taste for human novels. A hob in the market traded them to Cardan for roses smuggled out of the royal gardens.

Nearby, sprites wearing acorn caps and wielding glaives the size of toothpicks battled above a sea of tiger lilies. He glanced up to see Nicasia standing above him, a basket over her arm.

"I wish to talk," she said, and settled beside him, arranging a blanket and some little cakes dotted with dried fish and wrapped in kelp beside a bottle of what appeared to be a greenish wine. Cardan wrinkled his nose. There was no reason for her to go to all this trouble. It wasn't as though he hadn't behaved perfectly civilly toward her and Locke. The four of them menaced the rest of the Court as thoroughly as before. And if his cruelty had the sharp edge of despair, if slights and taunts were all that fell from his tongue now, what did it matter? He had always been awful. Now he was just worse.

"Have one," she offered.

If he wasn't going to rule by her side in the Undersea, he didn't have to eat the food there. "Perhaps once you've told me why you've disturbed my repose."

"I want you to take me back," she said. "None of our plans need to change. Nothing between us needs to change from the way it was before."

He yawned, refusing to give her the satisfaction of his surprise. Those were the words that he'd hoped for her to say when he'd discovered her with Locke, but now, he found he no longer wanted them.

In the end, he supposed Balekin had been right. Her dalliance had been a mere nothing. Balekin was probably also right when he said that only with her by his side would Cardan have some measure of political power. If he lost her, he was only himself, the despised, youngest prince.

Luckily, Cardan cared very little for politics. Or reprimands from Eldred.

"No, I don't think so," Cardan said. "But I am curious about your change of heart."

Out of the corner of his eye, he noticed one sprite tumbling into a flower and emerging heavily dusted with carrot-colored pollen. The other held up its glaive, victorious.

For a long moment, Nicasia didn't speak. She picked at a fishcake.

Cardan raised his eyebrows. "Ah, you didn't make the choice to leave him, did you?"

"It's more complicated than that," she told him. "And it affects you as well."

"Does it?" he inquired.

"You must listen! Locke's taken one of the mortal girls as his lover," Nicasia said, obviously attempting to keep her voice from shaking.

Cardan was silent, his thoughts thrown into confusion.

One of the mortal girls.

"You can't expect me to pity you," he said finally, voice tight.

"No," she said slowly. "I expect you to laugh in my face and tell me that it's no more than I deserve." She looked out toward Hollow Hall, miserable. "But I think Locke means to humiliate you as much as he does me in doing this. How does it look, after all, to steal your lover and then tire of her so quickly?"

He didn't care how it made him look. He didn't care in the least.

"Which one?" Cardan asked. "Which mortal girl?"

"Does it matter?" Nicasia was clearly exasperated. "Either. Both."

It shouldn't matter. The human girls were insignificant, nothing. In fact, he ought to feel delighted that Nicasia had such swift cause to regret what she'd done. And if he felt even angrier than he had before, well then, he had no cause. "At least you will have the pleasure of seeing what the Grand General does when Locke inevitably mishandles this situation."

"That's not enough," she said.

"What then?"

"Punish them." She took his hands, her expression fierce. "Punish all three of them. Convince Valerian he'd like tormenting the mortals. Force Locke to play along. Make them all suffer."

"You should have led with that," Cardan told her, getting to his feet. "That I would have agreed to just for fun."

It wasn't until he was glaring down at Jude, standing waist-deep in river water, fighting the current, that he realized he was in trouble. Ink swirled around her from the pot Valerian had dumped out. Sharp-toothed nixies lurked not far off.

Jude's wet chestnut hair was plastered to her throat. Her cheeks were flushed with cold, her lips turning bluish. And her dark eyes blazed with hatred and contempt.

Which was fair, he supposed, since he was the reason she was in the water. Valerian, Nicasia, and even Locke jeered from the bank.

Jude ought to be cowed. She was supposed to bow and scrape, to submit and acknowledge his superiority. A little groveling wouldn't have gone amiss. He would have very much liked it if she begged.

"Give up," Cardan said, fully expecting she would.

"Never." Jude wore an unnerving little smile in the corners of her mouth, as though even she couldn't believe what she was saying. The most infuriating part was that she didn't have to mean it. She was mortal. She could lie. So why wouldn't she?

In this, there was no winning for her.

And yet, after he told her all the soft, menacing things he could think of, after he left her clambering

back up onto the riverbank, he realized he was the one who had retreated. He was the one who backed down.

And all through that night and for many nights after, he couldn't rid his thoughts of her. Not the hatred in her eyes. That he understood. That he didn't mind. It warmed him.

But the contempt made him feel as though she saw beneath all his sharp and polished edges. It reminded him of how his father and all the Court had seen him, before he had learned how to shield himself with villainy.

And doomed as she was, he envied her whatever conviction made her stand there and defy him.

She ought to be nothing. She ought to be insignificant. She ought not to matter.

He had to make her not matter.

But every night, Jude haunted him. The coils of her hair. The calluses on her fingers. An absent bite of her lip. It was too much, the way he thought about her. He knew it was too much, but he couldn't stop.

It disgusted him that he couldn't stop.

He had to make her see that he was her better. To beg his pardon. And grovel. He had to find a way to make her admire him. To kneel before him and plead for his royal mercy. To surrender. To yield.

Choose a future, Balekin had commanded him when he'd first brought Cardan to Hollow Hall. But no one chooses a future. You choose a path without being certain where it leads.

Choose one way and a monster rends your flesh.

Choose another and your heart turns to stone, or fire, or glass.

Years later, Cardan would sit at a table in the Court of Shadows while the Roach taught him how to spin a coin over his knuckles, to set it whirling and have it land the way he wished.

Cardan tried again and again, but his fingers wouldn't cooperate.

"Tails, see?" The Roach repeated the movement, making it look frustratingly easy. "But a prince like yourself, what possible reason would you have to learn a rogue's trick?"

"Who doesn't want to control fate?" Cardan answered, setting his coin to spinning again.

The Roach slammed his hand down on the table, breaking the pattern. "Remember, all you really get to control is yourself."

X

The King of Elfhame Tries to Do One Good Thing

The night before they are set to meet with the solitary fey in the mortal world, Vivi and Heather take them out for bubble tea. There are no actual bubbles. Instead, he is served toothsome balls soaked in a sweet, milky tea. Vivi orders grass jelly, and Heather gets a lavender drink that is the color of the flowers and just as fragrant.

Cardan is fascinated and insists on having a sip of each. Then he eats a bite of the half-dozen types of dumplings they order—mushroom, cabbage and pork, cilantro and beef, hot-oil chicken dumplings that numb his tongue, then creamy custard to cool it, along with sweet red bean that sticks to his teeth.

Heather glares at Cardan as though he bit the head off a sprite in the middle of a banquet.

"You can't eat *some* of a dumpling and put it back," Oak insists. "That's revolting."

Cardan considers that villainy takes many forms, and he is good at all of them.

Jude stabs the remainder of the bean bun with a single chopstick, popping it into her mouth and chewing with obvious satisfaction. "Gooh," she gets out when she notices the others looking at her.

Vivi laughs and orders more dumplings.

When they return to Heather's apartment, they watch a movie about a terrible family in a big, old house and the beautiful and clever nurse who inherits everything. Cardan lies on the rug with one arm propping up his head and the other slung across Jude's waist. He understands everything and nothing he sees on the screen—just as he understands everything and nothing about being here with her family. He feels like a feral cat that might bite out of habit.

Oak gave up his room so they could sleep there, and although the bed is small, Cardan cannot mind when he takes Jude in his arms.

"You're probably missing your fancy palace right about now," she whispers to him in the dark.

He traces the edge of her lip, runs his finger over the soft human hair of her cheek, pausing on a freckle, and comes to rest on a tiny scar, a line of pale skin drawn there by some blade.

He considers explaining how much he despised the palace as a child, how he dreamed of escaping Elfhame. She knows most of that already. Then he considers reminding her that the fancy palace is now as much hers as his. "Not in the least," he says instead, and feels her smile against his skin.

But once he starts recalling his desire to leave Elfhame, he can't help but also recall how desperately she wanted to stay. And how difficult that had been, how hard she had fought, how hard she was still fighting, even now that she didn't have to.

"Why didn't you hate everyone?" he asks. "Everyone, all the time."

"I hated you," Jude reassures him, bringing her mouth to his.

Late the next afternoon, Bryern comes to the woods between the highway and Heather's apartment complex.

Jude's old employer turns out to be a phooka in a vest and a bowler hat. He has black fur, golden goat eyes, and what Cardan believes to be a bad attitude. He's accompanied by a scruffy clurichaun and a nervous-looking ogre serving as bodyguards, which suggests that Bryern was afraid to come before his sovereigns. That doesn't bother Cardan—in fact, he's rather pleased about it—but it's insulting to think those two would keep Bryern safe from the High

King and Queen of Elfhame. Not only that, but Cardan finds their bows to be insufferably shallow.

They seem rattled when they realize who he is. And somehow he finds that to be the thing that annoys him most of all, that they thought he wouldn't be bothered to come, that he would leave this to Jude.

His queen is dressed in mortal clothing, jeans and what they call a hoodie, her thumbs through holes at the wrists. Her hair falls mostly loose, but two braids hang near her face in a style she might wear in Elfhame, but which here does not mark her as anything other than a mortal girl who grew up in a mortal home.

For his part, he is clad in what Vivi told him to put on—black shirt and jeans, boots and jacket. No silver or gold except the rings on his fingers, which he refused to remove. He has never before willingly worn such an understated costume.

"So," Jude says, "you want to give me my old job back."

Bryern has the good sense to flinch a little. "Your Majesty," he says, "we are in the middle of a very difficult situation. A Court from the Northwest has come here, saying they are hunting a monster, and will not respect our self-governance. Their knights force us into servitude, claiming we must fight at their side. And the monster slaughters anyone who comes into the woods where it dwells."

"Huh," says Jude. "Where exactly are these w—"

"Which Court?" Cardan interrupts, hoping to keep Jude from immediately volunteering to fight something.

"That of Queen Gliten, Your Majesty," Bryern tells him, but then turns to Jude, fishing a folded paper out of his pocket. "This is a map. I thought you might want it."

Queen Gliten. Cardan frowns. He knows something about her, but he can't quite recall what.

Jude pockets the map.

Bryern gives an awkward bob of his horned head. "I wasn't sure you'd come."

She gives him a look that Cardan would not enjoy having leveled in his direction. "Is that why you compared my foster father to Grima Mog and tried to guilt me into it?"

"A comparison you can hardly mind, since Grima Mog now sits in a place of honor by your side," the clurichaun puts in hopefully, speaking for the first time.

"Stuff it, Ladhar," Jude says with a roll of her eyes. "Okay, we're on it. Don't say the High Court never did anything for you."

That night, Cardan lies in bed, looking at the ceiling, long after Jude falls asleep.

At first, he thinks it is the unfamiliar scents of this world keeping him awake, the iron tang that hangs over everything. And then he thinks that perhaps he has become too used to velvet coverlets and mattresses piled up on one another.

But as he slides out of bed, he realizes it isn't that.

After their meeting with Bryern, Jude was entirely amenable to his suggestions. Yes, they should immediately send a message to Queen Gliten and command her representatives to present themselves to be reprimanded. Yes, absolutely, they ought to send for reinforcements. And sure, he could look at the map, although it was tucked into her rucksack, so maybe he should look later. After all, they had time.

Heather cooked something she called "plant-based meat" for dinner, formed into the shape of "hamburgers" and dressed with two sauces, leaves, and slices of raw onion soaked in water. Oak ate two. After dinner, Cardan found himself at a picnic table outside, drinking rosé wine from a paper cup and laughing over every detail Vivi supplied about Madoc's attempts to fit into the mortal world.

It was an entirely lovely night.

Marriage means sharing each other's interests, and since his wife's run toward strategy and murder, he's used to her throwing herself at absolutely everything that crosses her path. If she isn't doing that now, there's a reason.

He pads out to the kitchen and takes her leather rucksack. Fishing around, he draws out the map from Bryern. Beside it, he finds the ancient leafy metal armor that Taryn—of all people—discovered in the royal treasury.

He shakes his head, sure now of her plan.

Sometime before dawn, she will wake, dress herself in that armor, strap on her mortal father's sword, sneak out, and go fight the creature. That's what she always planned, why she wanted to come without retainers or knights in the first place.

It would serve her right if he sat at the kitchen table and caught her as she tried to sneak out.

But when he takes the map to the window and reads it by the dim light of the streetlamp outside, he realizes something else.

Over the stretch of woods where the creature is supposed to dwell is marked *ASLOG*. And that's when he remembers the last time he heard Queen

Gliten mentioned—she was the one who cheated the troll woman out of what she'd earned. Now Aslog is being hunted, both by Queen Gliten's Court and by Jude, if she has half a chance.

Maybe he has the power to fix this. Maybe he's actually the only one who can.

Oak looks up sleepily from the couch he's been exiled to, but upon seeing Cardan, he turns over, kicking the blankets off his feet and burrowing deeper into the cushions.

XI

The King of Elfhame Gets What He Deserves

Cardan has seldom navigated the mortal world alone and finds himself fascinated by the strangeness of the landscape. The road stretches out in front of him, sand and slag and crushed stone bound in stinking oil. He passes closed grocery stores, hairdressers, and pharmacies with lights still on. Everything reeks of iron and rot, but in a way, he minds less and less as he grows more accustomed to being here.

He has put on one of Vivi's hoodies over his clothes, strapped Jude's sword across his shoulders, and glamoured himself both to hide the sword and to pass for human.

Although he has the map from Bryern, he quickly realizes it has no street signs and assumes a level of familiarity with the area that Cardan doesn't possess. After a few confused turns, he heads toward a gas station in the hopes of getting better directions.

Inside, a television is on, broadcasting the Weather Channel above a bored-looking, silver-haired clerk. Snacks sit beside electric cables, along with three refrigerators full of cold drinks and frozen dinners. A shelf of local delicacies features bags of saltwater taffy and something called crab boil. A spinner rack full of used paperbacks, mostly thrillers and romances, rests in the middle of the center aisle. Cardan browses with a lazy turn of his hand. One novel, titled *The Duke's Duke*, with a photo of a shirtless man on the cover, rests beside sequels: *Too Many Dukes* and *Duke, Duke, Goose*. Another book, *The Sleepy Detective*, features a drawing of a single closed eye.

What Cardan doesn't see are maps.

"Your pardon," he says, approaching the man behind the counter, intending to glamour him. Jude isn't there to be upset by it, and he could ask the man questions that would be highly suspicious otherwise. But with Aslog so much in his thoughts, he can't ignore his memories of Hollow Hall and the horrors of the ensorcelled servants there. He decides he will rely on humanity's intrinsic strangeness and hope for the best. "Might you have some means by which I can navigate your land?"

"Ayuh." The man reaches into a cabinet where cigarettes and various medicines are locked. He takes out a folded paper—a map, three years out of date. "Not many people in the market for these anymore, what with phones. We stopped ordering 'em new, but you're welcome to take this."

Cardan smooths it out on the counter and tries to spot where he is and where he's going, comparing this map with the memory of Bryern's scrawled and unhelpful document.

The clerk points to paperback books stacked up near the gum and candy. Their covers are purple, with cartoonish dead trees and a title in a

dripping-blood font. "If you're looking for interesting spots in the area, I wrote this myself and am my own publisher, too. *A Guide to the Secret Places of Portland, Maine.*"

"Very well, sir, I shall have it." Cardan congratulates himself on his skill at passing for human.

And if it seems as though the man mutters something about flatlanders as he rings up the purchase, well, whatever *that* is, Cardan is certain it has nothing to do with the Folk.

Of course, he has no human money. But the High King of Elfhame refuses to pay with glamoured leaves, as though he were some common peasant. He hands over glamoured gold instead and walks out with his purchases, feeling smug.

Under the streetlight, he flips through the man's book. An entire section is given to alien abduction, which he wonders whether Balekin might be responsible for—years passing in what seemed like hours was a common result of the memory-mangling that followed ensorcellment.

He learns about a ghost who haunts a busy street in town, drinking deeply of beer and wine when patrons' backs are turned. *Ladhar*, he guesses. He flips past tales of ghost ships and one of a mermaid rumored to sit on the rocks and sing sailors to their doom.

Finally, he comes to the place Aslog has made her lair—William Baxter Woods. Cardan isn't sure how long she's been there, but after finding two stories about a witch at its heart, he supposes a few years, at least. Apparently, a trail once ran straight through the center of the woods, but rangers closed it after three joggers went missing.

With a map full of street names, it doesn't take him long to find his way to the forbidden trail, hopping a fence and skittering down a ravine.

Once inside the woods, the air itself seems hushed. The sounds of car engines and the perpetual electric hum of machines drop away. Cardan removes his glamour, glad to be free of it, drinking in the fragrance of moss and loam. The moonlight shines down, reflecting off leaf and stone. He walks

on, his step light. Then he catches a new scent, burning hair.

When he spots Aslog, she is leaning over two stones—her massive body bent as she rotates one above the other in a makeshift mill, from which a fine white powder drifts. Beside it, he spots a worn and dented grill—like something stolen from a pile of rubbish. She has furnished the area with rusted porch chairs and an old sofa from which mushrooms grow. Along the forest floor, Cardan spots discarded clothing.

"Kingling," says the troll woman. "Here, in the mortal world."

"I was equally surprised to find you here, Aslog of the West. I wonder what changed that Queen Gliten hunts you so fiercely. Surely it isn't whatever you're doing here." He waves vaguely toward her eerie operation.

"I have added bonemeal to my bread," Aslog says. "Ground just as fine as any grain. My loaves will be more famed than ever before, though not for the same reason. And if I served Queen Gliten the bones of her own consort, at her own table, what of it? It is no more than she deserves, and unlike her, I do pay my debts."

He snorts, and she looks at him in surprise.

"Well," he says, "that's awful, but a little bit funny,

too. I mean, did she have him with butter or jam?"

"You always did laugh when you would have been better served staying silent," she says with a glower. "I recall that now."

Cardan doesn't add that he laughs when he is nervous. "I've come here to make you an offer, Aslog. I am not my father. As the High King, I can force Queen Gliten to give you the land you were cheated out of, although that will not save you from the consequences of all you have done since. Still, I can help if you'll let me."

"What are a few mortals to you? You never struck me as caring much for humans—until you took one for your bride. You never struck me as caring much for anything."

"You told me that stories change," he says. "And boys along with them. We are both different than we were at our last meeting."

"Once, there was nothing more that I wanted than what you're offering me. But it's too late. I am too much changed." The troll begins to laugh. "What have you got there on your back? Not a weapon, surely. You're no warrior."

Cardan regards Jude's sword with some embarrassment, the truth of Aslog's words obvious. He gives a long sigh. "I am the High King of Elfhame. I raised an isle from the bottom of the sea. I have strangled a dozen knights in vines. I hardly think I need it, but it does make me look rather more formidable, don't you agree?"

What he doesn't say is that he's brought it to slow Jude, lest she wake early and misread this situation.

"Come and sit with me," Aslog says, gesturing to one of the chairs.

Cardan crosses to it. Three steps and the ground gives way beneath him. He has only seconds to berate himself for foolishness before he hits the floor of the pit trap, metal chair crashing on top of him. All around him is a thin dusting of shining black particles. He inhales, then coughs, feeling as though he's choking on hot embers.

Iron.

He pushes the chair off, getting to his feet. The metal bits cling to his clothing, touch his skin with tiny ant bites of fire.

Jude wouldn't have made a mistake like this, he is dead certain. She would have been on guard from the moment she entered the woods.

No, that isn't right. Jude is on guard every hour of every day of her life.

Not to mention that iron wouldn't have slowed her in the least.

If he gets himself killed like this, she is never going to let him live it down.

"Even the High King cannot withstand iron," Aslog says, walking toward the pit, peering down at him. Above her, he can see the trees and the bright, full moon, a shining coin of silver spinning through

the sky. The first blush of sunrise on the horizon is still a ways off, and from this angle, Cardan may not even see it.

The troll woman bends and comes back up with a long pole. It looks as though someone has taken a rake and replaced the head with a black spike. She kneels down and uses it to stab at him as though she's a spearfisher after a marlin.

She misses twice, but the third strike scrapes his shoulder. He drops out of her range, holding the chair between them as a shield.

Aslog laughs. "It steals even your power, kingling."

Heart beating hard, lying in the dust of the iron filings, he reaches out with his magic. He can feel the land, can still draw something from it. But when he reaches toward the trees with his will, intending to bring their branches toward him, his control slips. The iron dust dulls his abilities.

He reaches the tendrils of his magic out again and sees the branches shiver, feels them dip. Perhaps if he concentrates very hard...

Aslog shoves her makeshift spear at him again. He uses the seat of the chair to block it, making the metal clang like a bell.

"This is silly," he says to Aslog. "You've trapped me. I can't go anywhere, so there's no harm in talking."

He rights the rusty chair and sits, dusting off as many of the iron filings as he can from his person, no matter how they scorch his hands. He crosses his legs, deliberately casual.

"Is there something you wish to say to me before I spear you through?" she asks, but does not strike. "You came to my woods, kingling, and insulted me with your offer of justice. Do you think it is only Queen Gliten whom I wish to punish? Your father might be dead, but that means someone else must inherit what I owe him."

He takes a deep breath. "Let me tell you a story."

"You?" she says. "A story?"

"Once upon a time," he says, looking up. His shoulder is throbbing. He feels like a child again, like the boy in the stables. "There was a boy with a clever tongue."

"Oh ho!" She laughs. "This is familiar."

"Perhaps," he says with a smile that he hopes will disguise his nerves. He thinks about the way Locke told stories, inventing them as he went, spinning them in the direction that might best delight the listener, and hopes desperately he can do the same. "Now, the boy lived on an island where he made a nuisance of himself, finding ways to belittle people that made them hate themselves, but hate him more. He was awful to the village maidens, favoring his wit over kisses. Perhaps he had reasons to be awful, perhaps he was born bad, but no matter. None of it gave him much pleasure, so he went into the woods where a troll woman lived and begged her to turn his heart to stone."

"That's an interesting variation," she says. She looks pleased, though, and drags one of the rusted, creaking chairs to the edge of the pit, settling herself in it amiably.

"He was angry," Cardan says, this part coming easily. "And a fool. Thereafter, he could feel neither pleasure nor pain, not fear nor hope. At first, it seemed like the blessing he had supposed it would

be. With a heart of stone, he had no reason to stay in his village, and so he took up what few possessions he had and set off across the sea to seek his fortune.

"Eventually, he landed at a town and found work doing labor for a tavern—carrying barrels of ale into the earthen root cellar along with carts of onions, wheels of cheese, turnips, and bottles of a thin and sour wine that the tavernkeeper watered down for guests. He was the one sent to break the necks of chickens and toss out drunks who could no longer pay for another round. He was paid little but allowed to sleep on the hard wood next to the dying fire and given as many bowls of greasy soup as he could eat.

"But as he lay there, he overheard two men speaking about an unusual contest. A wealthy warlord sought someone to marry his daughter. All one had to do was pass three nights in her company without showing fear. Neither man was willing to go, but the boy resolved that since his heart was stone, he would, and pass his life in ease."

"A warlord?" The troll woman looks skeptical.

"That's right," he affirms. "Very violent. Possibly making war on so many people was how his daughter wound up under a curse."

"Do you know why the Folk can tell stories?" she

asks, leaning forward and causing rust to fall around her chair. Her huge body makes it look sized for a child. "We who can never tell a lie. How can we do it?"

She speaks as though she supposes he's never asked himself that same question, but he has. Many times, he has.

Cardan tries not to let his nerves show. "Because stories tell *a* truth, if not precisely *the* truth."

She sits back, mollified. "Be sure yours does, little king, or it will dry up in your mouth, along with my patience."

He tries not to let that rattle him as he goes on. "That night, he told the tavernkeeper exactly what he thought of him and walked out, making another enemy for no reason at all.

"He took his boat from the dock and made for the warlord's land. When he arrived, the warlord looked him up and down, then shook his head, already certain of the boy's fate. Still, he would allow him to try to break his daughter's curse. 'If you spend three nights with her, then you will marry and inherit all I possess,' the warlord told him. Looking around the massive estate, the boy thought that wealth would bring him, if not pleasure, then at least idleness.

"But as evening came on, the boy was aware of

the strangeness of feeling nothing at all. He ate food finer than he had ever tasted, but it brought him no enjoyment. He was bathed and dressed in clothing more elegant than he'd ever seen, but he might as well have worn rags for all the satisfaction it gave him. He had begged for the heart of stone, but for the first time, he felt the weight of it in his chest. He wondered if he *ought* to be afraid of what was to come. He wondered if there was something profoundly wrong with him that he could not.

"As night fell, he was led to a chamber with a curtained bed. He walked around the room and noted the way the plaster of the walls was scarred with claw marks. He pulled back the coverlets, and feathers flew out in a cloud to dust the floor. As he discovered what seemed eerily like a bloodstain on the rug, she entered, a monster covered in fur, her mouth filled with razor-sharp teeth. It was only his heart of stone that kept him rooted in place, although he was almost certain he had heard the door being bolted behind him. He knew that if he ran, he was dead.

"They stayed like that for a while, the boy uncertain whether she would attack him if he moved, and the monster seemingly waiting for some sign of fear. Finally, the boy approached her. He touched the light fur of her jaw, and she leaned against his palm, rubbing her head like a cat." Cardan pauses. The story is almost at an end, and he has to keep Aslog listening a little longer. He wishes he could see the edge of the horizon, wishes he could tell the time by it, but all he has to judge the hour by is fading starlight. "They sat together through the night, the monster curling up on the rug and the boy gazing down at her. For though he had known the magic of the troll woman's curse, he had never known magic like this. Though his heart was as hard and cold as ever, he wondered what he would feel were it not.

"Finally, the boy fell asleep, and when he woke, the household was in an uproar. None of the other suitors had made it through a single night with the monster. They fussed over him, but when he asked questions about the monstrous bride, no one was particularly forthcoming. And so he set off to walk the estate and discover what he could on his own.

"On the far end of the land, he found a small house with an old woman planting herbs. 'Come and help me plant,' she said. But the boy was still awful, and he refused, saying, 'I wouldn't help my own mother plant, so why should I help you?' The old woman looked at him with cloudy eyes and said, 'It is never too late to learn to be a good son.' And without any answer for that, he planted her herbs. When they were done, in lieu of thanks, she told him that the girl had been raised to make war like her father, but when she wished to put down her weapons, he would not let her. And when the boy asked if the warlord had cursed his own daughter, the old woman would say no more.

"The second evening went much as the first. The monster roared in his face, but the boy didn't flee or cry out in terror, and they passed the night amicably."

"Let me guess," the troll woman says. "The third night goes swimmingly, too. His curse is broken and so is hers. They marry and live happily ever after, and the meaning of the tale is that love redeems us."

"You don't think monster girls and wicked boys deserve love?" Cardan asks her, his own heart kicking up a beat as he notes how few stars are visible. If he can just keep her talking a little longer, they may make it through this enterprise.

"Is this a story about people getting what they deserve?" the troll woman asks.

"Wait and see," Cardan says. "On the second day, the boy walked the grounds again and once more came upon the old woman's house. This time she was mending blankets. 'Come and help me mend,' she said. But the boy refused, saying, 'I wouldn't help my own sister with her mending, so why should I help you?' The old woman narrowed her eyes as though she saw his stone heart and told him, 'It is never too late to learn to be a good brother.' And without any answer for that, he sat down and helped her with her mending. When they were done, in lieu of thanks, she told him that she was a witch and that she was the one who put the curse on the girl, but only because the girl asked to be so powerful that her father could no longer control her. But the warlord had threatened the witch and forced her to alter the spell she'd cast so that if he could find a man to pass three nights with her and not be afraid, then the girl would be forced to obey her father thereafter."

The troll woman's brow furrows.

"By the third night, the household was in a state

of giddy anticipation. They dressed the boy like a bridegroom and planned for a wedding at dawn. The warlord appeared, praising the boy's mettle.

"But as he waited for the monster to come on the third night, he thought over what he knew of the girl and of the curse. He considered his stone heart and the clever tongue that had done little but get him into trouble. He knew he had lost the possibility of happiness, but he also knew her suffering would never touch him. He could live in riches and comfort. But it would never give him what he had already lost.

"And when she came through the door, he screamed."

"He's a fool," the troll woman says.

"Ah, but we knew that already," Cardan agrees. "You see, he realized he didn't have to *feel* fear. He only had to *show* fear. And since his heart was stone, he wasn't afraid of what would come next. He decided to take a chance.

"You know what happened next. She knocked him into the wall with a single heavy blow. And as he hit, he felt something crack in his chest."

"His heart," the troll woman says. "A shame he had to feel the terror, along with the agony of his own death."

Cardan smiles. "A great swell of fear crashed over him. But along with it was a strange and tender feeling for her, his monster bride.

"'You have cured me,' the boy told her, tears wetting his cheeks. 'Now let me keep your curse from ever being broken.' And she paused to listen.

"He explained his plan. She would marry him, and he would vow to never pass three nights without being a little afraid. And so the monster girl and the awful boy with the clever tongue marry, and she gets to stay powerful and monstrous and he gets his own heart back. All because he took a chance."

"So that's the lesson of the story?" the troll woman asks, rising from her rusty chair.

Cardan stands, too. "Everyone finds different lessons in stories, I suppose, but here's one. Having a heart is terrible, but you need one anyway.

"Or, here's another: Stories can justify anything. It doesn't matter if the boy with the heart of stone is a hero or a villain; it doesn't matter if he got what he deserved or if he didn't. No one can reward him or punish him, save the storyteller. And she's the one who shaded the tale so we'd feel whatever way we feel about him in the first place. You told me once, stories change. Now it's time to change your story.

"Queen Gliten cheated you, and the High King would not listen to your complaint. You didn't get what you deserved, but you don't have to live inside that one story forever. No one's heart has to remain stone."

Aslog looks up at the sky and frowns down at him. "You think you've made your story long enough for the sun to rise and catch me unawares, but you're wrong. And it will take only a few moments to kill you, kingling."

"And you think it was sunrise I was waiting for and not my queen. Do you not hear her footfalls? She has never quite managed the trick of hiding them as well as one of the Folk. Surely you've heard of her, Jude Duarte, who defeated the redcap Grima Mog, who brought the Court of Teeth to their knees? She's forever getting me out of scrapes. Truly, I don't know what I would do without her."

Aslog must have heard the tales, because she turns away from the pit, searching the woods with her gaze.

In that moment, Cardan reaches out to the land with his will. Blunted as his powers are by being in the mortal world and by the bits of iron that still cling to him, he is still the High King of Elfhame. The great trees bend their branches low enough for him to grasp one and swing out of the pit.

As soon as his feet touch the ground, he lifts the troll woman's abandoned chair.

Aslog turns to him in astonishment. He doesn't hesitate. He slams the rusted legs into her stomach, sending her sprawling backward into the pit.

An agonized howl rises as her skin touches the generous dusting of iron at the bottom.

As she stands, Cardan draws Jude's sword from his back. He points Nightfell toward the troll woman. "No part of that was a lie, save for the whole," he says with an apologetic shrug.

Aslog looks around her pit, her fingers scraping the roots and dirt along the sides. She is larger than Cardan, but not so big that she can clamber out unaided. She has set her trap well, crafting it to suit any of Queen Gliten's knights. "Now what?"

"We wait for the sun together," he says, his gaze going to the hot blush of the horizon. "And no one dies."

He sits with her as red turns to gold, as blue edges out black. He sits with her as gray creeps over Aslog's skin, and he does not look away from the betrayal on her face as she becomes stone.

Cardan lets himself fall back on the grass. He lies there for a long, dizzy moment, until he hears the tinkling of the leaves on Jude's armor. He looks up to see her running toward him.

"*What is wrong with you?*" she shouts, falling to her knees by his side. Her hands go to his shirt, pushing it aside to look at the wound on his shoulder. Her fingers are cold against his flushed skin. It's nice. He hopes she won't take them away. "You told *me* not to come alone, and yet here *you* are—"

"I knew Aslog," he says. "We were friends. Well, not precisely *friends*. But something. We were something. And I decided to play the hero. See how it felt. To try."

"And?" she asks.

"I didn't like it," he admits. "Henceforth, I think we should consider our roles as monarchs to be largely decorative. It would be better for the low Courts and the solitary Folk to work things out on their own."

"I think you have iron poisoning," she tells him, which could possibly be true but is still a hurtful thing to say when he is making perfect sense.

"If you're angry with me, it's only that I executed your mad plan before you got a chance," he points out.

"That's absolutely untrue." Jude helps him stand, propping herself under his good shoulder. "I am not so arrogant as to have begun my fight with a troll in the *middle of the night*. And I definitely wouldn't have managed to talk her to death."

"She's not dead," Cardan objects. "Merely imprisoned in stone. In fact, that reminds me. We need to alert our retainers to haul her back to Elfhame before sunset. She's probably rather heavy."

"Oh, *rather*," Jude agrees.

"You didn't hear the story I told," he goes on. "A shame. It featured a handsome boy with a heart of stone and a natural aptitude for villainy. Everything you could like."

She laughs. "You really are terrible, you know that? I don't even understand why the things you say make me smile."

He lets himself lean against her, lets himself hear the warmth in her voice. "There is one thing I did like about playing the hero. The only good bit. And that was not having to be terrified for you."

"The next time you want to make a point," Jude says, "I beg you not to make it so dramatically."

His shoulder hurts, and she may be right about the iron poisoning. He certainly feels as though his head is swimming. But he smiles up at the trees, the looping electrical lines, the streaks of clouds.

"So long as you're begging," he says.

Acknowledgments

This was a strange and magical project from start to finish, and a lot of people helped me get it right.

First, I have to thank my agent, Joanna Volpe, for figuring out how this book could work; my editor, Alvina Ling, for getting on board with such a weird project; and our art director, Karina Granda, for shepherding it through the many steps to getting it in front of you. Thanks to Ruqayyah Daud and Jordan Hill for managing so many details and also managing me.

Thank you to Siena Koncsol and everyone in Marketing and Publicity at Little, Brown Books for Young Readers, who have always been a joy to work with.

Thanks to Emma Matthewson and everyone at Hot Key Books for being enthusiastic about this series from the beginning.

Thank you to Rovina Cai for being willing to do this in the first place and then for putting up with me constantly asking for more Cardan extravagance.

Thank you to my critique partners for all your help. Thank you to Kelly Link for reading seventy thousand versions of this, to Cassandra Clare and Joshua Lewis and Steve Berman for convening a workshop with what was no doubt annoying swiftness, to Sarah Rees Brennan for helping me figure out what might happen in the first place and then helping me figure it out again when I went in a totally new direction, and to Leigh Bardugo for coming in and reminding me what a plot is and what I could do to suggest there was one.

And thank you to Jessica Cooper for letting me know what the people would like.

And, as always, thanks to Theo and Sebastian, for being both inspiration and distraction.

Sharona Jacobs

HOLLY BLACK

is the #1 *New York Times* bestselling author of fantasy novels, including the novels of Elfhame, *The Coldest Girl in Coldtown*, the Spiderwick Chronicles, and her adult debut, *Book of Night*. She was a finalist for an Eisner Award and the Lodestar Award and the recipient of the Mythopoeic Award, a Nebula Award, and a Newbery Honor. Her books have been translated into thirty-two languages worldwide and adapted for film. She currently lives in New England with her husband and son in a house with a secret library. Her website is hollyblack.com.

Rovina Cai

ROVINA CAI

is a freelance illustrator who received the World Fantasy Award for best artist. She works out of a cozy studio in Melbourne, Australia, in an old building that was once a convent and is possibly haunted.

Turn the page for a preview of

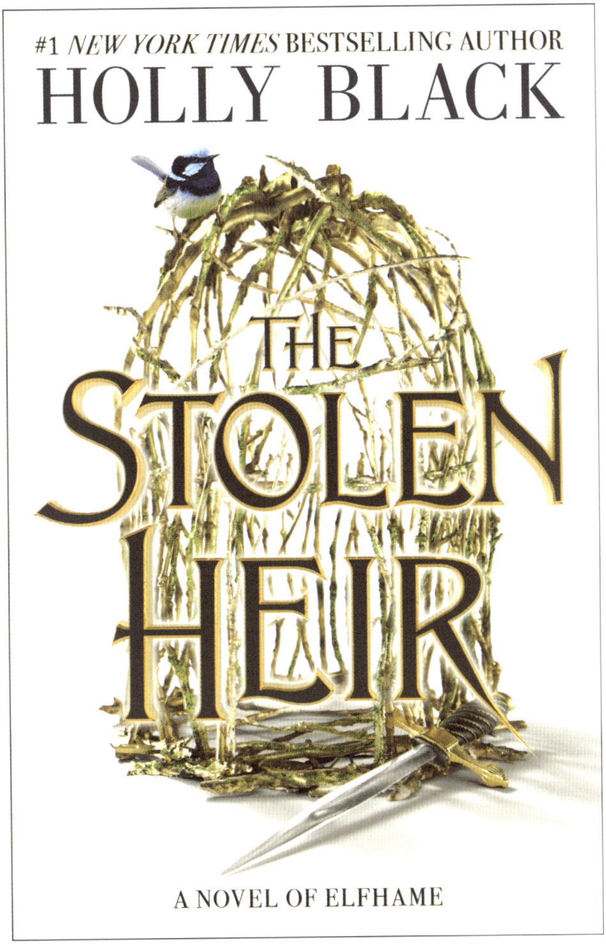

AVAILABLE NOW!

PROLOGUE

A passerby discovered a toddler sitting on the chilly concrete of an alley, playing with the wrapper of a cat-food container. By the time she was brought to the hospital, her limbs were blue with cold. She was a wizened little thing, too thin, made of sticks.

She knew only one word, her name. Wren.

As she grew, her skin retained a slight bluish cast, resembling skimmed milk. Her foster parents bundled her up in jackets and coats and mittens and gloves, but unlike her sister, she was never cold. Her lip color changed like a mood ring, staying bluish and purple even in summer, turning pink only when close to a fire. And she could play in the snow for hours, constructing elaborate tunnels and mock-fighting with icicles, coming inside only when called.

Although she appeared bony and anemic, she was strong. By the time she was eight, she could lift bags of groceries that her adoptive mother struggled with.

By the time she was nine, she was gone.

As a child, Wren read lots of fairy tales. That's why, when the monsters came, she knew it was because she had been wicked.

They snuck in through her window, pushing up the jamb and slashing the screen so silently that she slept on, curled around her favorite stuffed fox. She woke only when she felt claws touch her ankle.

Before she could get out the first scream, fingers covered her mouth. Before she could get out the first kick, her legs were pinned.

"I am going to let you go," said a harsh voice with an unfamiliar accent. "But if you wake anyone in this house, you will most assuredly be sorry for it."

That was like a fairy tale, too, which made Wren wary of breaking the rules. She stayed utterly quiet and still, even when they released her, although her heart beat so hard and fast that it seemed possible it would be loud enough to summon her mother.

A selfish part of her wished it would, wished that her mother would come and turn on a light and banish the monsters. That wouldn't be breaking the rules, would it, if it was only the thundering of her heart that did the waking?

"Sit up," commanded one of the monsters.

Obediently, Wren did. But her trembling fingers buried her stuffed fox in the blankets.

Looking at the three creatures flanking her bed made her shiver uncontrollably. Two were tall, elegant beings with skin the gray of stone. The first, a woman with a fall of pale hair caught in a crown of jagged obsidian, wearing a gown of some silvery material that wafted around her. She was beautiful, but the cruel set of her mouth warned Wren not to trust her. The man was matched to the woman as though they were pieces on a chessboard, wearing a black crown and clothes of the same silvery material.

Beside them was a huge, looming creature, spindly, with mushroom-pale skin and a head full of wild black hair. But what was most notable were her long, clawlike fingers.

"You're our daughter," one of the gray-faced monsters said.

"You belong to us," rasped the other. "We made you."

She knew about *birth parents*, which her sister had, nice people who came to visit and looked like her, and who sometimes brought over grandparents or doughnuts or presents.

She had wished for birth parents of her own, but she had never thought that her wish could conjure a nightmare like this.

"Well," said the woman in the crown. "Have you nothing to say? Are you too in awe of our majesty?"

The claw-fingered creature gave an impolite little snort.

"That must be it," said the man. "How grateful you will be to be taken away from all of this, changeling child. Get up. Make haste."

"Where are we going?" Wren asked. Fear made her sink her fingers into her bedsheets, as though she could hang on to her life before this moment if she just gripped hard enough.

"To Faerie, where you will be a queen," the woman said, a snarl in her voice where there ought to have been cajoling. "Have you never dreamed of someone coming to you and telling you that you were no mortal child, but one made of magic? Have you never dreamed about being taken from your pathetic little life to one of vast greatness?"

Wren couldn't deny that she had. She nodded. Tears burned in the back of her throat. That's what she had done wrong. That was the wickedness in her heart that had been discovered. "I'll stop," she whispered.

"What?" asked the man.

"If I promise never to make wishes like that again, can I stay?" she asked, voice shaking. "Please?"

The woman's hand came against Wren's cheek in a slap so hard that it sounded like a crack of thunder. Her cheek hurt, and though tears pricked her eyes, she was too shocked and angry for them to fall. No one had ever hit her before.

"You are Suren," said the man. "And we are your makers. Your sire and dam. I am Lord Jarel and she, Lady Nore. This one accompanying us is Bogdana, the storm hag. Now that you know your true name, let me show you your true face."

Lord Jarel reached out to her, making a ripping motion. And there, underneath, was her monster self, reflected in the mirror over her dresser—her skimmed milk skin giving way to pale blue flesh, the same color as buried veins. When she parted her lips, she saw shark-sharp teeth. Only her eyes were the same mossy green, large and staring back at her in horror.

My name isn't Suren, she wanted to say. *And this is a trick. That's not me.* But even as she thought the words, she heard how similar Suren was to her own name. Su*ren*. Ren. Wren. A child's shortening.

Changeling child.

"Stand," said the huge, looming creature with nails as long as knives. *Bogdana.* "You do not belong in this place."

Wren listened to the noises of the house, the hum of the heater, the distant scrape of the nails of the family dog as it pawed at the floor restlessly in sleep, running through dreams. She tried to memorize every sound. Her gaze blurry with tears, she committed her room to memory, from the book titles on her shelves to the glassy eyes of her dolls.

She snuck one last pet of her fox's synthetic fur and pressed him down, deeper under the covers. If he stayed there, he'd be safe. Shuddering, she slid out of the bed.

"Please," she said again.

A cruel smile twisted up the corner of Lord Jarel's face. "The mortals no longer want you."

Wren shook her head, because that couldn't be true. Her mother and father *loved* her. Her mother cut the crusts off her sandwiches and kissed her on the tip of her nose to make her giggle. Her father cuddled up with her to watch movies and then carried her to bed when she fell asleep on the couch. She knew they loved her. And yet the certainty with which Lord Jarel spoke plucked at her terror.

"If they admit that they wish for you to remain with them," said Lady Nore, her voice soft for the first time, "then you may stay."

Wren padded into the hall, her heart frantic, rushing into her parents' room as if she'd had a nightmare. The noise of her shuffling feet and her ragged breaths woke them. Her father sat up and then startled, putting an arm up protectively over her mother, who looked at Wren and screamed.

"Don't be scared," she said, moving to the side of the bed and crushing the blankets in her small fists. "It's me, Wren. They did something to me."

"Get away, monster!" her father barked. He sounded frightening enough to send her scuttling back against the dresser. She'd never heard him shout like that, certainly never at her.

Tears tracked down her cheeks. "It's *me*," she said again, her voice breaking. "Your daughter. You love me."

The room looked exactly as it always had. Pale beige walls. Queen-size bed with brown dog fur dirtying their white duvet. A towel lying beside the hamper, as though someone had thrown and missed. The scent of the furnace, and the petroleum smell of some cream used to remove makeup. But it was the distorted-mirror nightmare version, in which all those things had become horrible.

Below them, the dog barked, sounding a desperate warning.

"What are you waiting for? Get that thing out of here," her father growled, looking toward Lady Nore and Lord Jarel as though he was seeing something other than them, some human authority.

Wren's sister came into the hall, rubbing her eyes, clearly awakened by the screaming. Surely Rebecca would help, Rebecca who made sure no one bullied her at school, who took her to the fair even though no one else's little sister was allowed. But at the sight of Wren, Rebecca jumped onto the bed with a horrified yelp and wrapped her arms around her mother.

"Rebecca," Wren whispered, but her sister only dug her face deeper into their mother's nightgown.

"Mom," Wren pleaded, tears choking her voice, but her mother wouldn't look at her. Wren's shoulders shook with sobs.

"*This* is our daughter," her father said, holding Rebecca close, as though Wren had been trying to trick him.

Rebecca, who'd been adopted, too. Who ought to have been exactly as much theirs as Wren.

Wren crawled to the bed, crying so hard that she could barely get any words out. *Please let me stay. I'll be good. I am sorry, sorry, sorry for whatever I did, but you can't let them take me. Mommy. Mommy. Mommy, I love you, please, Mommy.*

Her father tried to push her back with his foot, pressing it against her neck. But she reached for him anyway, her voice rising to a shriek.

When her little fingers touched his calf, he kicked her in the shoulder, sending her to the floor. But she only crawled back, weeping and pleading, keening with misery.

"Enough," rasped Bogdana. She yanked Wren against her, running one of her long nails over Wren's cheek with something like gentleness. "Come, child. I will carry you."

"No," Wren said, her fingers winding themselves in the sheets. "No. No. No."

"It is not meet for the humans to have touched you in violence, you who are ours," said Lord Jarel.

"Ours to hurt," Lady Nore agreed. "Ours to punish. Never theirs."

"Shall they die for the offense?" Lord Jarel asked, and the room went quiet, except for the sound of Wren sobbing.

"Should we kill them, Suren?" he asked again, louder. "Let their pet dog in and enchant it so that it turns on them and bites out their throats?"

At that, Wren's crying abated in astonishment and outrage. "No!" she shouted. She felt beyond the ability to control herself.

"Then hear this and cease weeping," Lord Jarel told her. "You will come with us willingly, or I will slay everyone on that bed. First the child, then the others."

Rebecca gave a little frightened sob. Wren's human parents watched her with fresh horror.

"I'll go," Wren said finally, a sob still in her voice, one she couldn't stop. "Since no one loves me, I'll go."

The storm hag lifted her up, and they were away.

Wren was discovered in the flashing lights of a patrol car two years later, walking along the side of the highway. The soles of her shoes were as worn as if she'd danced through them, her clothing was stiff with sea salt, and scars marred the skin of her wrists and cheeks.

When the officer tried to ask her what had happened, she either wouldn't or couldn't answer. She snarled at anyone who came too close, hid beneath the cot in the room they brought her into, and refused to give a name or an address as to where her home had been to the lady they brought with them.

Their smiles hurt. Everything hurt.

When they turned their backs, she was gone.

NOVELS OF ELFHAME
ENTER THE WORLD OF FAERIE....
THE CRUEL PRINCE
#1 NEW YORK TIMES BESTSELLING AUTHOR
HOLLY BLACK
THE WICKED KING
THE NEW YORK TIMES BESTSELLING SERIES BY
HOLLY BLACK
THE QUEEN OF NOTHING
THE NEW YORK TIMES BESTSELLING SERIES BY
HOLLY BLACK
HOW THE KING OF ELFHAME LEARNED TO HATE STORIES
THE #1 NEW YORK TIMES BESTSELLING SERIES BY
HOLLY BLACK
Illustrated by ROVINA CAI
THE LOST SISTERS
A Novella of Elfhame
THE NEW YORK TIMES BESTSELLING SERIES BY
HOLLY BLACK
DIGITAL NOVELLA
#1 NEW YORK TIMES BESTSELLING AUTHOR
HOLLY BLACK
THE STOLEN HEIR
A NOVEL OF ELFHAME
#1 NEW YORK TIMES BESTSELLING AUTHOR
HOLLY BLACK
THE PRISONER'S THRONE
A NOVEL OF ELFHAME
BOB1152
LITTLE, BROWN AND COMPANY
NOVL

MORE FAERIE NOVELS

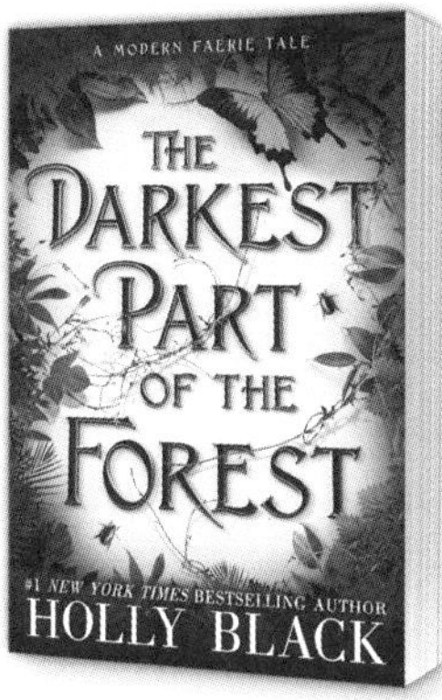

MORE DARK FANTASY

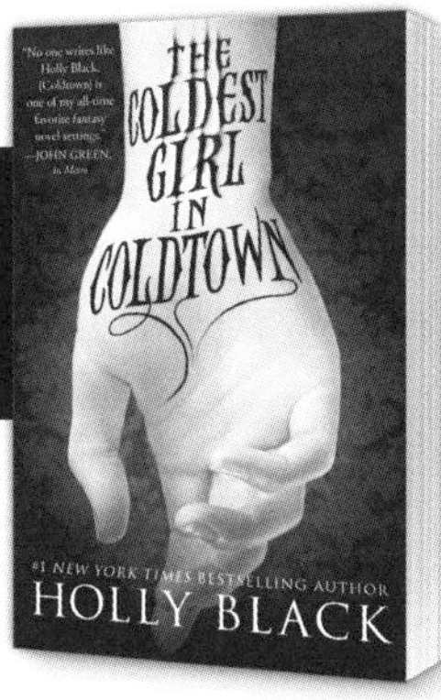